# Sword of Empire
## *Emperor*

RICHARD FOREMAN

First published 2014 by Endeavour Press Ltd.

This edition published 2018 by Sharpe Books.

ISBN: 9781723710346

# CONTENTS

# SWORD OF EMPIRE
Emperor

# 1.

Years of soldiering had marked his body and soul but Rufus Atticus still retained his aristocratic bearing and handsome features. He turned the heads of not just the whores who worked at the inn but some of the locals too. In particular he attracted the attention – and instant dislike – of Adminius Meriadoc, the son of the local chieftain. Adminius eyed the stranger with suspicion as he engaged Harbon, the mole-faced owner of the inn.

"Afternoon. I'm looking for an old friend of mine, who I believe lives in the area. His name is Quintus Verus," Atticus amiably remarked, despite being fatigued and soaked through. A young whore, Cordelia, gazed at the well-dressed and well-spoken newcomer with a suggestive expression. He looked like he might pay her double, though she would have gladly charged him half the fee should it have been in her power to do so. Jealousy now added fuel to the fire inside of the volatile Briton, Adminius. Before the stranger entered Cordelia had been eying him up. Adminius had had her last week – and he wanted her again.

"If he was any sort of friend wouldn't he have told you exactly where he lived?" Harbon replied, creasing his face up in scepticism. The stranger spoke the native language well but the innkeeper knew a Roman soldier when he saw one. But was he an officer or a deserter? Harbon was unsure whether to act with antagonism or deference towards the man who had just walked through his door.

"A fair point. But I can assure you I mean him no harm. Quintus will be pleased to see me, as I hope you're pleased to see me too."

The hawk-eyed Harbon caught a glimpse of the gladius beneath the Roman's cloak as he extracted a couple of silver coins from his purse and placed them on the counter.

"You'll need to head west, along the road to the next village. Ask for him there. He lives in a house on the northern outskirts of the settlement, I believe. I hope that you don't mean him any harm, for your sake." Harbon had once seen Verus get into a fight and he still winced when picturing what had happened to his opponents – or victims rather.

Atticus nodded and grinned, more confident than ever that Quintus Verus was indeed the man he was searching for. Atticus then creased his face – and nose – up at the pungent smell of stale beer, sweat and boiled vegetables permeating the air of the grim establishment. At least the smell was better than that of the stench of horse, dog and human excrement outside. The room was dimly lit but what the owner saved on lamp oil he didn't invest back into the décor. The light of Roman civilisation hadn't quite reached into this dark, dank corner of Britain, the centurion considered.

But people seldom came to the *The Black Stag* for the décor. People came for the drink, women and food – invariably in that order. The inn was half full, populated by farmers and tradesmen who had finished their work for the day. Some were red-nosed from years of drinking. Others were as tanned as leather from having spent a lifetime working in the sun (what little sun there was to be had on the sodden island).

"Two beers and some food please," Atticus said, removing another coin from his purse and glancing at the menu – a wooden board, filled with text and child-like drawings of animals.

"What would you like?" Harbon asked. Whether a deserter or officer the main thing was that the man's money was good.

"Whatever's fresh and tasty," the centurion replied, hoping that the establishment could at least meet one of those requirements. Atticus decided that his optio, Cassius Bursus, could choose his own meal once he finished securing the horses with the stable master next door.

Above the hiss of the slanting rain outside Atticus heard the sagging ceiling above his head creak – repeatedly. It seemed that one of the whores had already started work for the day. The soldier also heard the abrupt sound of a chair scraping along the floor. Then came a jangling noise as Adminius, wearing dozens of metal bangles on his arms, walked towards

Atticus. The nineteen year old possessed a lean build and spiteful expression. His long red hair needed washing and cutting. His red beard was slick with grease and redder in parts from wine stains. His cloak was made from a wolf's pelt and was fastened with a bronze brooch in the shape of a lion. A hunting knife hung down from his belt. Adminius Meriadoc looked like a man but too often behaved like a cruel, spoiled child.

"What's your business?" the Briton demanded. He slightly slurred his words and his eyes were glassy from drinking all afternoon. Adminius puffed out his chest, as best he could, and made sure that Cordelia was looking. He wanted to assert his manhood in front of the whore and also belittle the stranger. It was important that anyone new to the area realised the old order of things. Should the outsider have heard of the name of his powerful clan then he would rightly be intimidated by the son of the chieftain. If he hadn't heard of his family then it was about time that he did, having come into their territory.

"My business is just that – my business," Atticus replied evenly.

"I'm a Meriadoc. Adminius Meriadoc. Which means that any business this side of the river is also my business." Adminius swayed slightly as he spoke and poked himself in the chest. He had had too much to drink but Atticus suspected that the young Briton was just as unpleasant a character when sober.

"I'd advise you to sit down, before you fall down. Or before I knock you down." Atticus had walked into hundreds of inns similar to this one over the years – and nigh on all of them housed an Adminius Meriadoc in one form or another. It was best to put them in their place sooner rather than later.

"Ha, you and whose army?" The youth attempted to laugh off the insult.

The centurion was tempted to answer "Marcus Aurelius'" but he merely turned away from the Briton and perched himself upon a stool next to the counter.

"Are you ignoring me?" Spittle shot out from Adminius' mouth as he spoke. There was both bewilderment and anger in his voice – and the former fed the latter.

By ignoring him further the chieftain's son received his answer.

"Adminius, sit back down." The voice was gruff and authoritative and came from the corner where Adminius had been eating. A large plate of half-eaten dormice and chicken legs rested on the table in front of a fearsome looking Briton, as did a blood-stained short sword. Bardus Meriadoc was broader built and older than his companion but due to his fiery red hair and flat features Atticus rightly judged the man to be Adminius' brother. The brute's eyes were narrowed in either self-satisfaction or drowsiness. The brat can't handle his drink or his temper, Bardus thought to himself. He was also more concerned with dealing with his thirst and indigestion than picking a fight with a stranger at present.

"This is a wolf's pelt. I killed it myself, stabbing it in the heart," the youth snarled, baring his blackened teeth and moving closer towards Atticus.

The insouciant Roman was now equally as bored as he was amused by Adminius. He was tempted to either laugh or yawn in response to the adolescent.

"It's a dog eat dog world," he drily replied, little disguising his contempt for the Briton. Atticus could little disguise his dislike for the beer that the innkeeper had just served him either.

"You think you're funny?" The would-be bully snorted as he exhaled. The Roman could smell the drink on his breath. Adminius' blood was about to boil over, rather than just simmer. Yet still the centurion remained seated – and remained calm.

"You are far more amusing than I am, trust me."

Adminius was about to spit out a curse in the insolent newcomer's face when he was cut off.

"Sit down!" Bardus commanded. Instead of acting as one of the family's enforcers Adminius was behaving like a laughing stock. The stranger also had an air of danger, as well as calm,

4

about him. His younger brother was liable to take a beating, as much as that might do him some good. But should the man raise a hand to his kin then he would have to step in.

"He's insulting the family, Bardus," Adminius shouted back, whilst not taking his eyes off his antagonist. He knew that the locals were too scared of his clan to come to the outsider's aid – and if he somehow got into trouble then his brother would defend him. Bardus could swot the stranger like a fly, he believed.

"I'm not insulting your family, I'm insulting you. You're the one insulting your family." Before returning to the continent Atticus decided that he would recommend that the army should post a presence in the area. The Meriadoc clan needed to learn that they were not the law of the land. Rome was.

"How would you like it if I stabbed you in the heart?" A rictus of hatred formed itself across Adminius' face.

"You could try boy, but I worry that you'd end up blunting your knife. According to my ex-wife I've got a heart of stone." Atticus smiled, which only fuelled the Briton's ire – as the soldier knew it would.

Atticus couldn't be sure whether it was from someone nearby laughing at his joke or whether it was due to him calling the would-be warrior a "boy" – but the youth's blood finally boiled over. The Briton reached for his hunting knife, but no sooner did he clasp its cold bone handle then Atticus swivelled around on his stool and punched the youth in the throat. Adminius fell to the floor and gasped for air. He gazed up at the stranger with an expression of shock and fear.

The next thing to fall to the floor was Bardus' chair. He grunted, stood up and grasped his "lucky" short sword, as he called it. Atticus also noted the hand-axe tucked into his belt. *The people here are as hospitable as the weather.* The centurion drew his gleaming, sharpened gladius. *Kill or be killed.*

Customers moved out the way to give the two men a wide berth. If not for the spectacle of the prospective fight – and the attraction of seeing another Meriadoc being floored – the patrons of the *The Black Stag* would have retreated out of the door. Cordelia sighed and rolled her eyes, thinking how she had little chance of bedding either the handsome stranger or Adminius now. Silence ensued as the two men sized each other up. Patches of grey infected the Briton's red hair and beard, like mould, but Atticus judged Bardus to be a veteran warrior as opposed to a has-been.

The creaking sound which broke the eerie silence came, this time, from a bow rather than the ceiling or floorboards. The optio's arms were as muscular as a blacksmith's. Cassius Bursus, who upon joining the Praetorian Guard had been nicknamed Apollo due to his prowess with a bow, had entered the inn unnoticed when all eyes had been on Atticus and Adminius. Bardus took in the archer and recognised that the man knew his business. He'd killed before and could – would – easily kill again. The Briton reckoned that even if he were five times the distance away then the archer could still comfortably hit his mark. The brutal warrior hadn't survived this long without knowing when not to fight.

"You should realise that you've got more chance of having a whole week of sunshine than my friend here has of missing his target. I'd be more than happy for you to call my bluff, however. We'll take our leave. You can have a drink on me, though I suggest you have your kinsman sober up. He'll find it difficult to talk for the next few days but people will doubtless consider that a blessing as opposed to a curse. You're welcome to have the food I ordered too, as a punishment rather than a reward."

Bardus gripped the handle of his short sword tightly – and his face twitched in anger – but he nodded his head and conceded to the stranger's terms. He may have lost this battle but he would win the war, he vowed.

"Ride fast and hard. Because if I see you again I'll kill you."

"Funnily enough those were the last words my ex-wife said to me as well," Rufus Atticus wryly replied. The praetorian was tired, hungry and yet smiling – believing that he would soon be seeing his old friend again.

## 2.

A watery light trickled through the clouds. The rain, thankfully, had abated but a chill wind still scythed through their clothes and bones. Atticus and Cassius Bursus had now come off the main Roman road and were heading north along an inhospitable trail towards Quintus Verus' house. Carts had cut ruts into the narrow track. The mud sloshed beneath the hooves of their horses. An unpleasant, gaseous stench from a nearby bog assaulted their nostrils.

Rome, under Emperor Claudius, had invaded Britain in 43AD with the intention of mining vast deposits of gold and silver. Instead they had found rain and rebellion. Too much blood had been spilt and too much money had been invested in the campaign for it to fail, however. Horace called the inhabitants of Briton the "furthest of earth's peoples" but they were eventually brought into the fold of the Empire. Although it became apparent that the country was better suited for mining lead than gold, Rome encouraged other industries such as pottery, glass-making, textiles and the production of salt. Animal husbandry also increased, albeit in some parts of the west of the country there were rumours that farmers had taken their love of animals a little too far... Industry encouraged trade – and trade brought cultural exchanges, as well as the exchange of goods. The island grew more prosperous and diverse. Many leading Britons were conscious of educating their children in Latin and promoting the virtues of Roman civilisation. Some even wore togas. Roman baths and theatres sprung up across the country. But a civilising force was still an occupying force. As increasingly civilised as Briton was becoming, it had also been conquered. Rome constructed roads to transport goods and foodstuffs – and also troops and tax officials. Yet Britain was not just ill at odds due to its level of governance from Rome. Atticus had noticed how people from Londinium and the south-east of the island tended to look down their noses at the northern territories. The self-titled "elite" claimed to rule the rest of the country but they didn't always represent it.

"What sort of welcome do you think we'll get from Maximus?" Cassius Bursus asked. The archer had served under Gaius Oppius Maximus ever since the centurion had promoted him to the ranks of the Praetorian Guard nine years ago. The loyal soldier held his old commanding officer in high esteem – and wanted to keep things that way.

"Well hopefully we'll receive a better reception than we did back at the inn – although that won't be too difficult."

The truth was that Atticus didn't know how Maximus would react in response to encountering his old friends again. It had been five years since Maximus had disappeared. It had been five years since Maximus had found Aurelia, his wife to be, butchered in her own home. It had been five years since Maximus had killed the senator Pollio Atticus, Rufus' father – the man behind Aurelia's murder and also behind a plot to destroy the capital's grain supplies. It had been five years since the Emperor, supported by the physician Galen, had pronounced the centurion dead (in order not to condemn him as being a fugitive). *A lot can happen to a man in five years.*

And much had happened to Atticus during the past five years. He had been married, twice. His first wife had been Annia, the daughter of a prominent senator. Annia was uncommonly pretty but also uncommonly dull. Her conversation had been as stimulating as her lovemaking. He had tried to make things work – but failed. Atticus had partly chosen to marry her to make his mother happy, who had been devastated by the death of her husband.

"Some men are not cut out for soldiering, some men are not cut out for politics. I'm not cut out to be a good husband... Marriage is either a stage or a battlefield," he had confided in Cassius Bursus over a jug of Falernian one evening. Shortly afterwards Atticus divorced Annia – only to marry his mistress at the time, Valeria, a few months later. A wife and a family still seemed to provide the best solution for filling the hole in the praetorian's soul. Valeria made a better mistress than wife. As a mistress she had been fun, as a wife she was formidable.

Valeria was cruel to his slaves, vain and ambitious (both for herself and for her husband, who she kept pushing to sacrifice his military career in order to go into politics). "She was good in the bedroom but terrible in the kitchen... The only thing that I could trust her to cook up was an argument."

Valeria was also a drain on his finances, to such an extent that Atticus nicknamed her "the taxman" when he complained about her to his optio. "Her shopping trips are as long and costly as a military campaign." Over another jug of Falernian with his friend Atticus unburdened himself and resolved to get a divorce. "More than to my wife, I have to be true to myself... She's better off without me and I'll be better off, financially and otherwise, without her... I should just go back to doing what I do best and spend my nights in the company of other men's wives rather than my own."

During the past five years much had changed in the centurion's professional, as well as personal, life. Atticus had proved himself to be a trusted adviser and effective military commander to the Emperor. He was seldom absent from Marcus Aurelius' side on the battlefield or when negotiating diplomatic agreements. Atticus had also been instrumental in defeating Avidius Cassius in his bid to become Emperor.

"Do you think that this Quintus Verus will turn out to be Maximus then?" the optio asked. There had been false reports before. The Emperor always followed up on any rumour however, whether there was a sighting reported of him in Gaul or Alexandria, and sent one of his agents to investigate. The most recent report added up to more than just rumour though. A former legionary, who had set himself up as a wine merchant, had spotted Maximus at *The Black Stag*. The veteran, who had served in the same legion as Maximus, had sent a message to Atticus. The centurion passed the information onto the Emperor. The intelligence was up to date and from a trusted source. Marcus Aurelius had instructed Atticus and Cassius Bursus to journey to Britain.

"You're the only person who can bring him back Rufus... I would like to see Maximus again – before I die."

As famished as the centurion felt, the rumbling noise came from the distant thunder rather than Atticus' stomach. His horse moved its head from side to side, as if shaking his head in disbelief, like its rider, that the sky would be filled with rain again. The evening was drawing in, like a surgeon drawing a blanket across a corpse. The chill wind sang in the air with even greater spite. The soldier also heard the faint evening song of a thrush. Instead of being flanked by weeds and hedgerow Atticus noticed blackberry bushes and wild, winter flowers spring up along the track.

"We're about to now find out the answer to your question Cassius," Atticus replied, after a moment of silence. Both men stared into the distance and saw a house with its lights on. Their long journey was about to end – and another one was about to begin.

## 3.

The well-constructed two storey stone house was topped off with a wooden roof. Wisps of smoke spiralled out of the chimney. An out building of stables stood to the right of the property. Atticus also took in a vegetable garden and various animal pens which were home to chickens, pigs and goats (the latter of which bleated as the riders approached). He recalled how, around a campfire, Maximus had once declared that he wanted to own a farm – should he ever leave the army, and live the quiet – peaceful – life. But the centurion conceded that the second act to his life would probably live in the shadow of the first. His dreams as a farmer would be eclipsed by the nightmarish scenes he had witnessed during his career as a soldier. Nothing would be able to compete with the blood-pumping highs and lows of battle. "You can't help but feel alive, when life is a series of near-death experiences," Atticus had replied to his friend many years ago. "Drink will have to liven our spirits, or dull the ache, if we ever become farmers."

A figure, Dann, came out of the stables, carrying a rake, and walked towards Atticus and Cassius Bursus. The wizened old servant, wearing a moth-eaten woollen cloak over his tunic, was gap-toothed and bald. He eyed the strangers with a certain amount of chariness and moved his jaws, like a cow chewing upon cud.

"Evening. We're looking for Quintus Verus," Atticus said.

The servant tilted his head and scrutinised the two men even more stringently, hoping to divine their intentions in relation to his master. Before the Briton had a chance to open his mouth and respond though his master appeared before them, standing in the doorway to the main house.

"No you're not. You're looking for Gaius Oppius Maximus. But you won't find him. Because he's dead," Gaius Oppius Maximus said, flatly. It had been five years since the soldier had last said or heard his name.

Atticus smiled on seeing his former commanding officer. He thought that Maximus' voice sounded distinctly rougher compared to when he had last heard it. Grey hair coloured his temples, like the markings of an old wolf. His face was lined with age or sorrow – or more likely both. A black, bristling beard covered his jaw and neck. The farmer still retained a soldier's build, although Atticus could discern a slight pot-belly beneath Maximus' tunic. His down-turned mouth managed a half-smile on taking in his former comrades. His eyes smiled not, however. Cassius Bursus was surprised by Maximus' lack of surprise. Atticus had once considered the centurion as being akin to a block of iron. But the iron was now flecked – infected – with rust. Maximus' careworn, bloodshot eyes revealed how much drink was dulling the ache too.

Maximus asked Dann to attend to his guest's horses and invited them into the house. Atticus surveyed the clean but austere interior. The furniture was simple but sturdy. The only nod towards his homeland was a painting on the wall, depicting a scene from the Battle of Pharsalus where Maximus' antecedent, Lucius Oppius (the "Sword of Rome"), had fought for Caesar against Pompey in the civil war. But the ex-soldier's wants were few and his possessions even fewer, it seemed. Atticus recalled a comment by Marcus Aurelius, in reference to Maximus: "He's an even greater stoic than myself. And perhaps more Spartan than Roman." Atticus couldn't work out if his Emperor had spoken in jest, admiration or pity.

Despite having questions, despite not having seen his closest friend in five years, Maximus remained silent as he tossed a couple more logs onto the fire and lit an extra couple of the lamps hanging from the oak beams criss-crossing the ceiling. Atticus couldn't be sure if his old friend was glowering in the half light. Was there despondency, disbelief or indifference on his face?

"Would you like a beer?" their host asked, finally turning towards his guests.

Cassius Bursus nodded his head enthusiastically, puffing his cheeks out in relief and prospective pleasure.

"When in Briton, do as the Briton's do," Atticus replied.

Maximus poured out three large cups of the local brew. He also served his famished guests some ham and cheese. Cassius commented that he was so hungry that he would even eat the cuisine north of Hadrian's Wall.

"I'm afraid it doesn't quite look and taste as good as the stuff we drank in Egypt, but we've had worse."

The three comrades clinked cups, as they had done so a thousand times around campfires when campaigning against the northern tribes. Atticus peered over the rim of his cup. The liquid was about as transparent as a tax collector's accounts and he remembered, with even more fondness, the beers he had sampled when posted in Alexandria. They had been as golden as the inside of Cleopatra's jewellery box and as intoxicating as her perfume. The three men quickly gulped down the murky brew, however, as if it were the elixir of life, and the host brought over the jug to keep their cups re-filled.

They sat in a horseshoe around the fireplace. The beer helped warm the atmosphere too, although the air was still rife with shards of awkwardness. Maximus often looked at his two old friends but then said nothing. Rain began to spit across the wooden roof. The fire was bright but eerily silent. Atticus noticed how, when Maximus wasn't clasping his cup, he would fidget with the gold band he wore on the fourth finger of his right hand. The ring had been a gift from Aurelia. The inscription on the inside of the band read, "The light shines in the darkness." Maximus would often obsessively turn the ring on his finger, when in company or alone. The sensation reminded the praetorian of Aurelia – of her beauty, goodness and violent death. Maximus' soul had been blackened by so much grief over the years it was now incapable of letting light in or out. He had lost his first love to the plague, the second to politics. His heart was a small lump of coal, soaked in beer.

"So how did you find me?"

"Aelius Scaevola, an old quartermaster from the legion, spotted you in a nearby tavern and wrote to me," Atticus replied. *He's like a corpse that doesn't want to be dug up.*

"I always knew that my drinking would be the end of me," Maximus said, neither wholly joking nor wholly serious, as he thrust a poker into the fire and shifted the logs, to let the air in. "Did you come here for yourself, or were you sent?"

"Both. I wanted to see you. But the Emperor instructed me to find you. He wants to see you again Gaius. Before he dies."

Maximus paused but then spoke. "I've long since ceased giving or receiving orders, Rufus. Aurelius would be the first one to appreciate that we're all due to die. We've got more chance of civilising a tribe of Picts than changing that fact. Besides, the Emperor's a god. What does he need a mere mortal for? No. I won't be leaving here. He needs to let me live and die in peace. Tell him that I'm glad he'll finally find some peace too. Tell him also that I never blamed him for not pardoning me."

Maximus got up and threw another brace of logs onto the fire, which now started to crackle. The rain slapped upon the roof. Maximus had often thought of his Emperor – friend – during the past five years. He had left without saying goodbye or thank you. When news came through that Avidius Cassius was challenging Aurelius for the throne the centurion had been tempted to come back from the dead and fight by his general's side, one last time.

"You can tell him yourself. You can always return here afterwards, should you want to. But the Emperor and army would welcome you back. My father's influence in the Senate has died out. You'll be a hero, not a fugitive."

"I don't much feel like a hero. I'm content to remain here. I live comfortably. I'm seeing a return on my investment in a local mine and Dann looks after the farm. The wine and weather may be disagreeable, but you can get used to both after a while. How has Aurelius been over the past five years though?" Maximus asked. Concern shaped his features.

"I suspect that five years has felt like five lifetimes. His health has been as fragile as the peace with the northern tribes.

For all of the endless victories we've won, the war still rages on. It's a forest fire that keeps flaring up in different places. A piece of Aurelius died when Avidius Cassius looked to wear the purple, I think."

"His robes ended up red though, I understand. A centurion in his army assassinated him, before he could cause a civil war in earnest."

"Aye. But that's another story," Atticus answered, sharing a look with his optio as Cassius Bursus briefly paused whilst wolfing down his plate of salted ham and goat's cheese. "A greater piece of him died, however, when Faustina passed away. I must confess, I neither liked nor trusted the Empress. I've little doubt that she was Avidius' lover at some point. Yet Aurelius was still devoted to her, in his own way. When he honoured her, in his oration, Aurelius described Faustina as being "So submissive, so loving and so artless". Either he was being sarcastic, or blind. He was certainly wilfully blind before she died, refusing to read the correspondence she shared with Avidius. It probably would have incriminated her. Instead, he deified her. Aurelius also minted special coins with Faustina's image on, to commemorate her. She always did like to get into a man's pockets."

Maximus half-smiled at his friend's wit but also sadly remembered the Emperor's lack of judgement where his wife and son had been concerned.

"And what of Commodus?" Maximus asked, hoping that the boy had become a man – a good man.

Atticus shook his head in disappointment and disparagement. "I think of him as the son of Nero and Domitian rather than Aurelius, unfortunately. He plays the dutiful heir in front of his father but he's religiously cruel, vain and depraved behind his back. Aurelius invited Commodus on campaign and to accompany him during a tour of the east. He introduced him to scientists and philosophers, hoping to inspire and edify the youth. But he has more chance of edifying a Pict. Once his face appears on our coins the currency will instantly depreciate. He was given a consulship aged fifteen, the youngest ever. But should he live to fifty he would not merit such an honour. The argument is that he is the worst option in regards to wearing the purple, but he is also the only option. A bad Emperor is preferable to a civil war and power vacuum. I admire Aurelius deeply but instead of passing more powers onto his son – in preparation for his death – he should have passed them to the Senate for safekeeping. Commodus will turn the marble of Rome into mere rubble, I fear."

"This country's weather will prove a blessing, if it prevents Commodus from visiting this corner of the Empire. He'll try and burn bright – and then burn out. But I'd rather turn my attention to this boy, who became a man," Maximus remarked, proudly looking at Cassius Bursus. "You look older Apollo – but you still annoyingly appear less than half my age. How have you been? Has the archer been struck by Cupid's arrow yet? Are you married?"

"He's unfortunately been struck down with a few diseases from women over the years, but not that of love," Atticus said, smiling at his own joke.

The optio blushed and grinned at the same time, perhaps fondly remembering the encounters with the aforementioned women, regretting not a minute he had spent with them.

"I've been too busy attending Atticus' weddings to attend my own."

Maximus widened his eyes in astonishment. His mouth was agape too, though he was lost for words.

"It's true, believe it or not. I've been married and divorced – twice – in the past five years." Atticus smiled, imagining how surprised and amused his old friend would be at the news.

"I thought that you might be dead by now, but never married. What was it you used to say? Hades will freeze over before you shackle yourself to a wife, ruining your life and hers. Cupid must have an even better aim than you, Cassius, to have hit such a fleet-footed target. Divorced twice I can believe, but not married twice," Atticus said, smirking and shaking his head in disbelief. "So tell me, who did Rome's most eligible bachelor lose his heart to?"

"Well my second wife was called Valeria. And I lost my savings to her, as opposed to heart. For her part she called me conceited, flippant and unfaithful. I should have never let her get to know me so well."

Maximus laughed. It felt like it was the first time he had done so in five years.

Maximus' cheeks were flushed from sitting next to the fire but his eyes were red-rimmed from years of heavy drinking, Atticus noticed. He considered that his friend was cocooning himself in a permanent drunken stupor. He had observed politicians do it before, ones who were bitter at never having attained the high office that they thought they merited. Or he had known veterans to consciously drink themselves unconscious, in an attempt to help blot out the various atrocities they had witnessed or committed.

Cassius Bursus had turned in for the night. The optio was exhausted and he had been instructed by his centurion earlier to leave him and Maximus alone for part of the evening.

The occasional flame darted upwards from the low-burning, smouldering fire. A stale silence hung in the air between the two old friends. It was a silence encompassing both five seconds and five years. How much of Maximus was there left in the semi-retired farmer – the man who had just wearily declared that he was just killing time, before time killed him? Maximus sat, his head bowed down as if too heavy to lift up. Finally he spoke, after pouring the dregs of the jug of beer into his cup.

"I'm sorry that I lost your friendship, Rufus. But I'm not sorry that I killed your father, all those years ago." Sober or drunk, Atticus could always count on Maximus to be honest – sometimes brutally so.

"I grieved the loss of my friend rather than my father. He was willing to see Rome starve to feed his ambitions. He ruined my mother's life. He nearly ruined my sister's life. He might have ruined my life, if a certain centurion didn't take me under his wing. You never lost me as a friend. You gave me a second chance Gaius – and for that I'll always be thankful. I just want to now give you a second chance. Come back with me. The army – and Aurelius – are in Sirmium. You're slowly dying here."

*I'm already dead.* "It's not possible. Not even Galen could furnish me with a cure, a pick-me-up, for the way I feel. It's good to see you again, though, Rufus."

"Anything's possible. If I can marry, twice, then you can come back from the dead."

Maximus half-smiled. He recalled Aurelia reading her bible to him – about the story of Lazarus. Sometimes her ghost haunted him, sometimes it saved him.

"If I could bring anyone back from the dead, it wouldn't be me." Maximus thought of both Julia and Aurelia. Of Arrian too. They deserved to live far more than him.

Atticus bowed his head as well, weighed down by his friend's sadness. But he raised it again. "There's another reason why you need to come back with me."

"What is it?" Maximus replied, his voice weakened with tiredness and sorrow.

"You need to see your son."

Maximus and Atticus continued to stay up long into the night as the centurion told his friend about the baby that Claudia – Atticus' sister – had given birth to five years ago – nine months after Maximus had spent the night with her. Claudia had named the baby Marius, after her grandfather.

"He's good-natured and healthy. He has his father's eyes, but thankfully not his grey hair… Claudia divorced Fronto whilst pregnant but Aurelius has made sure that mother and baby have wanted for nothing… My sister has changed these past five years. She's a good mother. Her better nature has been given room to flourish, from having come out of the shadow of our father. By killing him, you let her live…"

There were tears in his eyes as Maximus tried to take everything in. Some of the tears were borne from remembering Lucius and Aemelia, his children from his first marriage who he had lost to the plague. But more so his tears were borne from the news that he had a son. Maximus felt guilty too, for not being there for his son and his mother. But he had not considered that Claudia would have had a child from their one night together. She had been instructed by Pollio Atticus to seduce Maximus. Maximus had in turn seduced Claudia, in order to pass on false intelligence back to her father.

"For years doctors told Claudia that she was unable to bear children. Galen delivered the baby. He called Marius a minor miracle... I know that he wasn't conceived in the most conventional circumstances but something good came of something corrupt. It just goes to show you, anything's possible," Atticus remarked, placing a fraternal hand on his friend's shoulder.

The rain stopped but the fire burned on. Maximus would see Aurelius once more. He would see his son, for the first time. He would even draw his sword again, if he had to...

Anything was possible.

## 4.

Maximus slept fitfully that evening. But rather than being kept awake by spectres from the past his thoughts turned to the hazy image of his young son. He found himself smiling, uplifted. He had been absent from his life for five years. He had a lot of catching up to do. That night Maximus also prayed to God. For years he had cursed his name, or denied his existence. But a chink of light shone through the clouds and Maximus asked God to keep him – and Marius – safe. He just wanted the chance to see his son (even just once) and to provide for him.

Despite going to bed late he still woke up with the dawn. A dapple grey fog encircled the farm. The chilly air misted up his breath as well. The ground was dusted with frost. Maximus called Dann in to speak to him, after the Briton had given out his orders to the three farmhands for the day. After a couple of years of service Maximus had rewarded his land manager with a share of his estate's holdings. He could be trusted to keep his business affairs in order. Maximus told the leather-faced Briton that he would be returning to the continent and the army again. The old man nodded, masticated, and looked impassive for the most part – but then grinned, gummily, when he heard the news that his master had a son.

"You are a man with a mission again," Dann croakily remarked. Maximus wasn't sure if he was referring to fatherhood or his prospective military service.

"Thank you. Should you encounter any trouble or difficulties you should see Algar. I'm about to write him a letter now."

Algar was the chief of a nearby tribe. He had made the Roman an honorary member of the tribe when he had first come to the region, many years ago. Algar was a descendant of Adiminus, a former chieftain of their tribe who had served with Lucius Oppius at the battles of Alesia and Pharsalus.

"Will you be returning before the spring?"

"Anything's possible," Maximus replied, after a thoughtful pause whilst surveying the landscape.

Atticus and Cassius Bursus slept in. When they woke Maximus said that he was keen to leave for the continent that day. They would ride to the nearest port and charter a ship to take them to Gaul. The optio sighed a little inside. His trip to the famous – or infamous – island was going to be all too brief. He had hoped that he could sample some of the women of Briton. He had heard good things about the busty serving girls. It was rumoured that they were happy to be taken advantage of, after a few drinks. So too he would be happy for them to take advantage of him, drunk or sober. But the itch would have to remain unscratched for now, unfortunately (the soldier was so desperate for the arms of a woman that he would have even taken one from north of Hadrian's Wall, he considered). They were homeward bound.

By midday the three companions were ready to leave. They were just waiting on one of the farmhands to finish saddling Maximus' horse. Such was the cacophony of noises from the livestock that maybe the animals intuited that their owner was going away. Maximus knew that he was as much leaving home as journeying towards one. After escaping from Rome he had felt that the best place to isolate himself from the world would be on the distant island. He would miss his drinking sessions with Algar, although he would not miss how he felt during the mornings afterwards. His days of being Quintus Verus hadn't been all bad.

But the farmer would have to become a soldier again. Maximus' sword felt heavy in his hand when he strapped it on, after five years. Dann had kept the blade oiled and sharpened, thinking that his master might have cause to use it again one day.

As the wizened land manager stared across the horizon – and saw over half a dozen armed horsemen approaching the house – he suddenly thought how that day might be today...

## 5.

The midday sun had evaporated the fog and melted the frost. Maximus counted eight riders, trotting in a row. He could also just about make out the swords and axes popping out over their shoulders from being strapped to their backs.

"Friends of yours?" Atticus asked, squinting in an attempt to better make out the figures in the distance.

"Doubtful. I'm not exactly renowned in these parts for throwing dinner parties."

Maximus noted his land manager jutting out his chin next to him and firmly grasping his pitch fork. No matter who his visitors were, however, it wouldn't be the old man's fight. Maximus instructed Dann to fetch his pair of hunting spears – and then head back inside. He also instructed one of his farmhands to lead the horses back into the stables. He didn't want the animals getting spooked or injured, should trouble ensue.

"I'll take care of our guests Dann, don't worry. Apollo – post yourself up on the roof. Stay out of sight until I give the order."

The optio nodded and nimbly climbed up the side of the house, stationing himself behind the stone chimney.

"Unfortunately they're friends of mine," Atticus remarked, as he gradually discerned the frame and features of one of the horsemen. *Bardus Meriadoc*. "I recognise two of them, Bardus and Adminius Meriadoc. I suspect that their companions are family members. We had a slight altercation at the tavern yesterday. I knocked Adminius on his arse and Cassius nearly had to put an arrow in Bardus. In my defence I did buy them a round of drinks afterwards to try and take the sting out of things."

"Well, at least you didn't sleep with someone's wife. That's progress I suppose," Maximus said, as he planted the two hunting spears in the ground between himself and Atticus.

He had thankfully had few dealings with the Meriadoc clan over the years. They had perhaps left him alone because of his affiliation with Algar – and he lived just beyond what they deemed was their territory. Their reputation preceded them, however. They had started – and ended – more blood feuds than Maximus could recall. The head of the family was Ammius. The self-proclaimed chief had carved out his position in the region through violence, theft and intimidation. He routinely paid off corrupt tax collectors and military officials – otherwise people paid him, through rent money, interest on loans or his own form of taxation. Cruelty was a source of amusement to Ammius, as well as part of his business plan. He possessed four wives and had fifteen children (most of them sons, as daughters were less of an asset to him). He would have possessed five wives, but his last wife had died a year ago. Some said that Ammius had murdered her for being unfaithful, while others claimed he had disposed of her because she was barren. As well as a cruel streak Ammius also liked to display his sense of munificence every now and then – and on certain feast days he would arrange large dinners and tournaments (which members of his own family invariably won). It was a chance for Ammius Meriadoc to give something back to the community, which he regularly extorted money from throughout the remainder of the year.

The stolidly built chief rode at the centre of the line of horsemen on a large, snorting black charger. He also rode slightly ahead of his men. The default position of his mouth was a sneer. The polished bronze torc around his neck reminded Maximus of the one which Ballomar, the leader of the Marcomanni, had worn at the Battle of Pannonia. Maximus also took in the rest of his unwelcome guests. They shared similar features: red hair, beetling brows, flat noses and dark eyes. The family resemblance (Ammius' "wolf pack", as he called them, were made up of his brothers, sons and nephews) was accentuated through bedraggled beards and the equally bedraggled furs they wore.

Ammius Meriadoc stopped and looked Maximus up and down, his lip curled in an even more pronounced sneer. At the same time Bardus took in Atticus. He bared his yellow teeth and blood-red gums in a goading, self-satisfied smirk. Adminius Meriadoc, wearing a scarf to cover the bruising on his neck, was also bright-eyed with spite. He was keen to say something Atticus, to show that he was having the last laugh, but his throat was still sore and he was unable to talk properly.

"You know who I am. You know why I'm here," Ammius stated bluntly in a guttural voice. "This man before you is a fugitive. He attacked a member of my family – and if you attack one Meriadoc you attack every Meriadoc. I will have recompense, Quintus Verus, either in gold or blood. I'll leave that choice to you. But either way I will not be leaving your farm empty-handed. Forgiveness is not an option. Mercy isn't a Meriadoc family trait."

"Neither is intelligence, it seems," Maximus said as an aside to Atticus.

"Or a sense of style, judging by what they're wearing," the centurion added. "Although, from the look of them, a love of incest may well run in the family."

Before replying to the brutal looking Briton Maximus was briefly distracted by a quartet of crows cawing to each other on a skeletal birch tree to the right of his house. Perhaps they were calling to one another – anticipating some entertainment, or a prospective feast. He also noted a couple of the men dismount and twirl their axes in their hands, in a bid to intimidate their quarry. One had a long neck like a giraffe and spat like a camel. The other had a broken nose, which seem to zig-zag and defy Euclidean geometry, Atticus fancied.

"I've got a counter proposal. How about I let you leave here with your life, instead of my friend or my gold?"

The Briton let out a laugh, or rather a cackle. But then he snorted, in the manner of his horse, and glowered at the Roman. Nobody spoke to Ammius Meriadoc in such a disrespectful manner. He would now take their lives and take their valuables. He could make a gift of the property to his soon to be married nephew.

"I thought that you Romans were accomplished mathematicians. I see eight of us and only two of you."

"Should you want to even the odds and make it a fairer fight we'd be happy to have you go back and collect more men," Atticus exclaimed, as his hand reached around his back to check that his pair of throwing knives were easily accessible beneath his layers of clothing.

Ammius was not the only Meriadoc to laugh this time.

"You're funny," Ammius remarked, slapping his hand across his leather-clad thigh. "Maybe I should enslave you, instead of kill you, and employ you as a clown to amuse my young children."

"Is his aim and arm still good?" Maximus quietly asked the centurion, referring to his optio.

"Aye, he's good. The kind of diseases he picks up only affect him below the waist. Should I be more worried about you? Do you still remember how to use that sword?" Atticus replied, not entirely in jest.

"I suspect that we're both about to find out."

The chief wiped the smile from his face and signalled to his two dismounted men (his younger brother and nephew) to attack the Romans. Bardus had asked his father that morning if he could be the one to kill the stranger who had disrespected the family, but Ammius had replied that if he was so keen to kill the man he would have done so on the evening before, without the support of the rest of the clan. Also, it had been some time since his brother and nephew had killed someone. Their axes needed to taste blood.

Cassius Bursus covertly surveyed the scene from behind the chimney. He controlled his breathing, nocked an arrow and waited for the order.

The Briton with the long neck and fondness for spitting let out a battle-cry and closed in on Atticus. He was fearsome and heavy-set but the centurion was willing to bet he was also slow. The axe swished through the air with little accuracy. Atticus stepped backwards.

The warrior with the broken nose attacked Maximus. His axe was modified and topped off with a spear point, which he jabbed forward at the Roman. Maximus sidestepped one of the thrusts, however, and moved inside. He whipped his elbow around to smash against his opponent's face – and shattered his left cheekbone. The dazed Briton was then easily despatched as Maximus jabbed his sword through his stomach.

The Briton grinned in pleasure, believing that he had the beating of his opponent. He soon grimaced in agony, however, as Atticus darted forward unexpectedly and sliced open his enemy's hand, which was gripping the weapon. The axe fell to the ground, as did the man shortly after.

"Apollo! Make it rain."

Maximus barely had the time to draw breath again, after bellowing his order, when the first arrow zipped through the air and punctured the lung of the man on the horse to the right of Ammius, who was about to launch his spear at Atticus. The shock for the Britons from witnessing their kin fall to the strangers was compounded by the appearance of the archer on the roof. Such was the speed with which the second shaft was released that for a moment it seemed that there may be more of the enemy raining death from above.

Ammius Meriadoc quickly unhooked the round shield on his saddle and placed it in front of him, just before an arrow thudded into the wood. Unfortunately his brother, to the left of him, was unable to retrieve his shield quickly enough to avoid the spear which Maximus threw into his sternum. Adminius emitted a hoarse cry – or squeak – of despair. His plan was to dismount and take cover behind his mare but he panicked and fell from his mount, spraining his ankle in the process.

Bardus decided that attack was the best form of defence. He kicked his heels into the flanks of his horse and aimed to mow down Atticus. The first of the centurion's throwing knives lodged itself into the Briton's shoulder. Atticus then leapt to his right to avoid the oncoming horse. He swiftly gained his footing and threw his second knife into Bardus' back, before he had the opportunity to wheel his mount around and attack again. The brawny warrior lost consciousness – and never woke up – as he slumped forward and his colt galloped on into the distance.

Ammius surveyed the battlefield. His sneer morphed into a snarl. He was tempted to flee. He would lose his pride and honour, but not his life. He had more sons at home, who could help replenish his forces in a dozen years or so. He could hire mercenaries in the interim to retain his power base in the region. All would not be lost. But a red mist descended before the Briton's eyes. The Roman must die, even if he was injured or killed in the attempt.

He yelled and rode towards Maximus with his shield in one hand and his axe in the other. The charger's hooves churned up mud. At first Maximus looked to retrieve his second hunting spear but Ammius anticipated his intention. All he could do was dive out the way, to the side where his opponent held his shield rather than his razor-sharp axe.

Cassius Bursus spotted the danger to Maximus and nocked an arrow. The experienced warrior skilfully wheeled his horse around whilst his enemy was still on the ground. The Briton observed the archer target him however, and he raised his shield accordingly to fend off the missile. But by concentrating on the archer and raising his shield Ammius exposed his mid-rift. Maximus firmly gripped his gladius but then let it fly out of his hand as he threw the sword at the warrior chief. The blade sheathed itself through Ammius' ribcage – piercing his heart.

Atticus stood over a pale, trembling Adminius. The slight but familiar metallic tang of flesh and blood began to lace the air, along with the smell of horses.

"You caused all this," the centurion remarked, unable to mask the contempt and melancholy in his voice.

"I promise, I won't cause any trouble again," the youth replied, his voice trembling as much as his body.

"I know you won't," Atticus said coldly, before plunging and twisting the blade of his gladius into the Briton's throat.

The crows cawed in the background even louder, as if applauding the spectacle.

Atticus watched his friend use the furs of his enemy to wipe the blood off his sword. The farmer had fought well. *Maybe he isn't that rusty after all.*

Cassius retrieved his arrows – and relieved the corpses of any valuables too.

27

Maximus sighed in exasperation at the waste of it all and the fact that, even before they had set off, they had encountered delays. *I just want to see my son.*

"What do we do now?" Dann asked his master, grinding his teeth and thinking. He gazed at their chief and bid good riddance to the Meriadocs. Life would go on, for the better, without them.

"They're dead. We bury them and act as if they were never here," Maximus said flatly – although he was tempted to feed some of the corpses to his pigs as a goodbye present to them.

## 6.

*Sirmium.*

Galen had seen enough death in his lifetime to know that his patient – and friend – was dying. The famed physician didn't need to check the Emperor's pulse to know that it was weak, but he did so anyway. How much was his exhaustion physical and how much was it spiritual? Only the gods knew – and they would remain mute.

The room was populated by various desks, stacked high with books, scrolls, maps and all manner of documents pertaining to up-and-coming legal disputes and diplomatic treaties. On a bedside table to his left stood several empty phials, which had contained a special theriac Galen had concocted to ease the Emperor's pain and help him sleep. The physician had increasingly added more opiates to the mixture, which had the effect of sometimes dulling his patient's wits, as well as his pain.

Marcus Aurelius was sitting up in bed, supported by several cushions. He had been offered the billet of the finest residence in the area but the commander was determined to remain with his men in an army camp on the outskirts of town. The engineers had constructed a house for their beloved general within a week. Galen forced a smile, in reaction to taking his friend's pulse. The physician noted how his ailing patient's beard was now more white than grey. His skin seemed so ashen and powdery Galen fancied that a strong gust of wind might blow the tired expression from the Emperor's face.

But the divine spark hadn't been completely extinguished. Death, or life, had not broken him quite yet. The stoic was determined to endure the world for a little longer. Aurelius wanted to expand the borders of the Empire to the Carpathian Mountains. The Germanic tribes needed to be subdued, once and for all. He wanted to see Maximus again. He also wanted to make sure that Commodus was ready and worthy to inherit the throne. In regards to the latter, Galen thought that Aurelius would have to live another lifetime, however. An eternity. Far more than the campaign against the northern tribes his son was a lost cause. The physician had seen the youth in the camp earlier, cavorting with a courtesan and her brother. The brother and sister were rumoured to cavort with each other too. *Caligula might even blush in the face of the boy's wicked and depraved temperament.*

"It looks like that the doctor will outlive the demi-god, no? I wouldn't want it any other way," Marcus Aurelius fondly remarked to his old friend. His voice was stronger than his pulse, but not by much.

"I'm sure that your name will outlive mine – and many others. Your book sales will doubtless eclipse mine too," Galen said, noting how his patient had barely touched his food – some cereal sweetened with honey – which sat on a table next to his bed.

"I might be tempted to lay a wager on the opposite being true, if I thought that I'd be around to collect on the bet. Plato posited that states flourish under rulers who are philosophers. I'm not entirely convinced. My reign may prove to be synonymous with an endless, unwinnable war and a plague which decimated the Empire. Or, for better or worse, I will merely be forgotten. But that's as it should be. Everything fades away and quickly becomes a myth; soon complete oblivion covers us over," Aurelius said. He appeared to be at ease, rather than despairing, at the bleak thought.

"You are being too harsh on yourself. I'm not usually one to agree with 'the people' as such, but they are right to speak well of your reign. Let us hope that you still have a future. The Empire needs you."

"The Empire needs an Emperor – and one who can fulfil his duties better than I can at present. I have had my time, Galen. Commodus will soon have his. I know that you have not always approved of him. He has his faults but some of them may be delivered at my door. I was an absent father for most of his life. His mother indulged him, which is a mother's prerogative. Since Faustina passed away I have tried to do too much too quickly," Marcus Aurelius said, his head bowed down in pensiveness, shame and fatigue. *But it's proved too little and too late.*

"I will at this rate remember you as a ruler who was too hard on himself," the sage physician warmly replied.

"Commodus was more concerned with visiting the arena than the lecture halls during our tour of the east unfortunately." *And visiting the brothels at night.*

"You did your best, Caesar." *But your best wasn't good enough, for once.*

"He fulfilled his duty and sat in on numerous legislative cases that I presided over, which is something." *And was more interested in metering out punishments, than justice.*

Galen could not bring himself to openly disagree with his Emperor. But he could not bring himself to openly support his misplaced judgements either. His silence said it all.

"I am optimistic that the throne will ennoble him. He may prove to be more of a warrior than a philosopher – but a warrior is what Rome may well need."

*He will prove to be more of a tyrant and sybarite than a warrior.* "What will be will be," Galen said, philosophically.

"Indeed. We cannot alter the past or future. Commodus will be an Emperor of his own making. I have learned that it is impossible to make a man exactly how one wishes him to be. If it were possible I would have created an army of men akin to Maximus and Atticus. If Atticus is able to locate the Maximus then I believe that he will return. How is Claudia and their son?"

"She has settled in well at the house in town you organised and sends her regards. The boy is in fine health too," Galen replied, retrieving several phials of theriac from his bag and putting them on the bedside table to his patient's right.

"Claudia is much changed from the woman she used to be, isn't she? And changed for the better. The responsibility of motherhood has made her see the world – and herself – in a different light. Perhaps the responsibility of office will change Commodus for the better. Where there's life there's hope, as Cicero used to say."

It was now the Emperor's turn to force a weak smile.

## 7.

Sunlight sliced through the gaps of the shutters, as did the smell of pine.

Cassius Bursus washed down the grapes he was eating with a fine Massic vintage. He was, along with Maximus and Atticus, riding in an imperial coach through Gaul. The son of a village farrier had come a long way, he thought to himself. Cassius had long appreciated his father for forcing him to practise archery as a boy all those years ago – but the soldier duly appreciated him again, and more.

The ride was one of the most agreeable experiences he had ever had travelling, due to the construction of both the road and the coach. He admired the gold leaf scroll work which decorated the inside of the coach. He also pocketed a gold coin he found in between two cushions – and called it a tax rebate. It was a welcome change, travelling in such style. He was used to being the escort, rather than the one being escorted – in this case by the squadron of cavalry accompanying them. Cassius idly wondered if Caesar had ever travelled along the same road he was on, when campaigning in Gaul. He promised himself that he would one day visit the town of Alesia, to take in the scene of Caesar's greatest victory.

Although the shutters were closed to keep out the wintery chill Maximus wore the expression of a day-dreamer and fixed his gaze at the window as if it were open. For the first hour or so of sitting in the carriage Maximus had sat on the opposing seat, as if looking back to Britain or the past. But he then wordlessly moved seats and Maximus now looked to Sirmium and the future. Occasionally his stony face would crack – and the hint of a smile would animate his expression.

"I instructed one of the cavalry to ride ahead and secure us rooms at an inn for the evening. Dinner will be on me too, or rather on the Emperor. It's refreshing to have some money in my pocket that my ex-wives don't feel entitled to," Atticus remarked in good humour, looking forward to a hot meal and warm bed.

"Despite the money they extracted from you Rufus, I can't help but think of your ex-wives as 'poor women' for being married to you," Maximus said, in equal good humour. "What prompted you to wed in the first place?"

"It made my mother happy. I also thought that I was in love, or told myself I was. And not in love in the poetical sense. Real love. But I was still as deluded as a poet. In the end, in regards to both wives, we were fonder of each other when we were apart. I guess I gave both of them handsome settlements out of guilt, for being unfaithful. I tell myself that I'm cursed with boredom. But really I'm just selfish. It could be worse though. I could be boring. I also married out of a desire to have a family. I may well have the odd child out there already, being brought up by the husband to the wife I slept with. But I wanted a family of my own. You need to be a good husband before you can be a good father though, unfortunately."

"I'm just hoping that you're a good map reader and we don't stray into enemy territory," Maximus said. He wanted to get to Sirmium quickly, but safely.

"The lines of the map have been redrawn over the past five years. There are fewer bandits and raiding parties along the border now. Many of our enemies are now friends, out of fear rather than love. My worry is for the plans to redraw the lines of the map even more. The Emperor is intending to expand the frontiers of the Empire to the Carpathian Mountains. The Goths may not prove to be the most amiable of neighbours. I'd trust them to keep the peace about as much as I'd trust a Gaul in a shield wall to advance."

"So why does Aurelius want to redraw the map?"

"You may want to ask him yourself. But I believe that he is trying to give his son one last gift, before he passes away. He wants to occupy the territory so Commodus will never have to refight his battles – although eventually we may have to fight new ones, against the Goths. Rather than sow salt into the land, as Rome did with Carthage, Aurelius plans to plant forts and soldiers across the province. But the plague has weakened the army and its recruiting pool. His imperial overreach will exceed his grasp. To garrison the northern territories the army will have to transfer soldiers from the likes of Britain and Egypt, which could destabilise those regions. The army cannot fight on multiple fronts. Not even the gods can be in two places at once. The army needs more men," Atticus posited, apprising his friend of the situation.

*I just want to see my son.*

## 8.

"You look a picture of happiness there Cassius, with that girl sitting on your knee," Atticus shouted across the table at the inn.

"Aye, but the reason why I'm happy is because she *isn't* sitting on my knee," the optio responded jovially, before giving the dimpled, raven-haired whore a sloppy kiss. Wine stained his chin. He breathed in her cheap perfume. The avuncular owner of the establishment had boasted that his girls were the cleanest in the province, but also the most filthy-minded. *The Golden Plough* possessed "the finest whores in all of Gaul, at a competitive price".

A large, stoked fireplace heated a room filled with travellers, merchants and officials. Lamps hung from the ceiling, as did a collection of various tankards. Colourfully dressed women, their eyes darkened with kohl and their faces red with mulberry juice, led men off to private rooms where they would make good on the claims written by satisfied customers on the toilet walls.

Many a woman tried to catch Maximus' eye – and even more of them wished to capture the attention and purse of his handsome companion. But the two friends were content just to talk to each other – and allow Cassius Bursus to have their share of any fun.

"So tell me more about Avidius' attempted coup," Maximus said, pouring himself another cup of wine. "I never had much regard for him, although I'm sure he didn't much care as he had plenty of regard for himself. He lost my respect when I heard that he punished a number of looting soldiers by crucifying them. He also mutilated deserters to serve as adverse advertisements for others who might be tempted to desert."

"Well in some respects he deserted his own post, by challenging rather than serving the Emperor. After receiving a report that Aurelius had died Cassius declared himself regent and Emperor. It's still unclear whether Faustina knew for sure or not that her husband was still alive, but initially she supported Cassius' bid to seize power. It was rumoured that she was willing to marry him to further strengthen his claim. On hearing the news of his friend's treachery Aurelius offered to pardon him. Cassius considered that it would have been un-imperial to abandon his claim. The self-titled demi-god wasn't keen on returning to being a humble soldier again, after pronouncing himself Emperor. He also proudly boasted that he was a second Catiline. Whilst looking to mobilize his legions in the east he also reached out to the Senate. Suffice to say they also didn't hold him in the high regard that he thought they should have. Soldiers, senators and the populace supported Aurelius. The would-be Emperor was armed with ambition, but little else. A friend wrote to Cassius and summed things up in just one statement, 'You are mad'. Aurelius prepared for war, although he was wary of dividing his forces too much and leaving the northern territories under strengthened. Thankfully he didn't have to."

"I heard that two of his own soldiers murdered him."

"They may have been two soldiers, but they were not his men," Atticus said knowingly, lowering his voice.

"Who were they?"

"Well one of them is sitting over there – with a girl on his lap – and the other one is sitting opposite to you."

Maximus' eyes were stapled wide. He shook his head in disbelief but then nodded it in approval. The praetorians clinked their cups and grinned.

"Well anything is fucking possible it seems. How many people know it was you?"

"Five. The Emperor, the agent who helped us infiltrate the legion, Apollo, myself – and now you. The agent insisted that we present the severed head of the enemy to the Emperor. To Aurelius' credit he refused to look. The Emperor punished a few conspirators who sided with Cassius, but most he pardoned."

Maximus inwardly recalled something Aurelius had said to him many years ago, after acquitting a servant accused of murdering his master. "There is nothing which endears an Emperor of Rome to mankind as much as the quality of mercy."

The two friends were interrupted in their conversation by the front door to *The Golden Plough* opening, bringing in a gust of cold air and Quintus Perennis, the officer in charge of their detachment of cavalry. Perennis briskly walked over to the centurion and stood to attention, his polished helmet, topped with a distinctive red plume, cradled under his arm.

"Our horses have been watered and fed, sir. Would you like me to assign you any men to act as guards for the evening?"

"Thank you Quintus, but we'll be fine. Although I fear, perhaps, that Cassius over there may have to fight off all the women at some point tonight, if he's not careful. Consider yourself off duty. Make sure your men are watered and fed – and that you turn some of the water into wine," Atticus remarked, whilst tossing the officer a small bag of coins to cover the expenses for the evening.

"Thank you, sir," the officer replied, unable to suppress a grateful smile. Perennis then turned to Maximus. "I just wanted to say to you, sir, that my men and I are pleased to see you back with us. It's an honour to serve alongside you again. I was there at the Battle of Pannonia."

Maximus was unsure what to say in response so he merely nodded and half-smiled.

*My war's over… I just want to see my son.*

## 9.

Commodus' chest glistened with oil. Titus and Sabine, brother and sister, lay either side of the soon to be Emperor. Commodus had claimed the villa that his father had declined to stay in. The property, in the centre of town, was far away from the prying eyes of gossiping soldiers or the judgmental looks of his father. Commodus idly thought to himself how he might paint his chest hairs gold, to match his fair hair (which he often decorated with flecks of gold dust). *The people like majesty.*

Braziers surrounding the large bed glowed and illuminated the painted figures on the walls of the bed chamber, who were looking on like voyeurs. There was a light in Titus' eyes too as he gazed at his lover with undisguised adoration. Commodus smiled back, pleased and recently pleasured. Titus' hair was slicked back and fragrant with myrrh. He was a former artist's model, praised for his beauty. His features – his almond eyes and pronounced cheek bones – were almost as feminine as his sister's.

Titus was twenty years old. Commodus was the first lover he had taken (or who he had let himself be taken by) who was older than him. Usually he shared the beds (and secrets) of senators, plutocrats and other powerful men. Titus enjoyed being desired. He was attractive, charming and ambitious. "We have to use every asset we have," the son of a stonemason often said to his sister.

Titus had wormed his way into the affections of the Emperor's son after catching his eye at a party. Commodus had bedded him that night and Titus had proved his worth as a lover and also as someone his companion could confide in and receive advice from. He told Commodus what he wanted to hear and, although no great wit himself, Titus knew when to laugh at other peoples' jokes. When they all eventually travelled back to the capital Titus would serve as the young Emperor's chamberlain. He would stand in the shadows by day and lie in his bed at night. His greatest ambition was to be the Second Man of Rome. He would be master over all those grey-beards who had once looked down on him and treated him like a slave or whore.

Commodus stroked Titus' face with his fingertips and bestowed a kiss upon his "Ganymede", as he sometimes affectionately called him. Commodus then turned to bestow his attention on the woman. His leg was hooked around hers beneath the covers. Sabine smouldered more than any brazier. Lovers drunk in the courtesan's perfume and alluring looks. Her sphinx-like pout could signify a hundred things – but most men only thought about one thing when they saw her. Sabine was five years older than her brother and an even more experienced lover and consort than her sibling. She could dress elegantly or provocatively, with equal accomplishment. She could act demurely or play the wanton. Different performances could be tailored to different audiences. Sabine knew what men wanted – and gave it to them. Desire was all about supply and demand; it was a commodity that could be manufactured and traded. She had been married twice, to men who had plenty of money but little time left to spend it. A piece of graffiti in Rome commented about the lauded beauty saying that, although she had never bored her husbands, she had eventually worn them out.

Commodus ran his hand through her long, luxuriant auburn hair. She rubbed her head against his palm, almost purring with pleasure. To amuse himself though, Commodus suddenly and spitefully pulled a few strands of hair out of her head. The woman yelped in pain and was about to curse the perverted teenager but she wisely reined herself in. Sabine knew she could ultimately lose her head, as opposed to just a few strands of hair, if she displeased the vindictive boy. She smiled and allowed him and her brother to laugh (giggle) at the joke. Sabine had seen Commodus' aspect both glow with sensual pleasure and flash with ire in the past. He had been violent with her before. Frustrated with not being able to climax one evening he had blamed the woman and slapped her, repeatedly. He drank too much, especially for one who couldn't hold his drink. Drink made his temper even more erratic. He would slur his words, vomit and grow glassy-eyed. The courtesan pouted and smiled but thought to herself how the incident was another reminder to her that she had to leave her current life behind. Her wealth could buy her freedom and independence. She had no wish to belong to anyone anymore – and that included being part of Titus' schemes. He behaved more like a pimp than brother nowadays.

*I don't want to be a trophy to be competed for anymore... I don't want to be the Emperor's wife or his mistress... I may even suffer blisters soon, from having to applaud everything the "young Hercules" does...*

Sabine was tired of pretending to love someone. She wanted to love and care for someone for real – whatever that meant. She had recently met someone who was different. He made her laugh and she felt freer, alive, when she was with him. But should that affair prove chimerical too then she was content to retreat from the world. Sabine may have been half as ambitious as her younger brother but she was more than twice as intelligent. She painted, read voraciously and spoke three languages. She had recently started to translate *The Aeneid* into Greek and had purchased a villa in Puteoli that was rumoured to have once belonged to Cicero.

*My life could be good.*

Commodus knew he would soon grow tired of the sister. She was a proficient rather than passionate lover. He was as fond of her as he was a pet dog, peacock or ostrich (all of which he had executed for his sport and amusement in the past). A courtesan is still just a tavern whore – but with a larger collection of shoes, he thought to himself. Her brother, however, would be a different story. Commodus valued the young man, who would soon be in his prime, for his eagerness to please and his counsel. He would need such devotees when he ruled the Empire: men who would wake up early for him and stay up late with him. Keep him entertained. His chamberlain could sign documents for him and sit in on legal disputes, but Commodus would sit in on sentencing hearings and pass judgement. He enjoyed witnessing the extreme

41

reactions on the faces of the guilty and innocent alike. Most people he would punish, severely. But in order to keep things interesting – and keep people guessing – he would pardon one in every ten defendants.

Already Titus acted as Commodus' agent, keeping him informed about who was an ally or potential enemy. He corresponded with senators on his behalf, procured suitable women and boys for his enjoyment and collected donations and bribes from clients who wished to benefit from the Emperor-in-waiting's favour.

Unfortunately Commodus had mostly received mere trinkets and promises over the past six months. He knew, however, that the real donations – and ability to extort funds – would come once he was Emperor in earnest. He needed money for both his coronation and his father's funeral – suffice to say he would devote more expenditure to the former rather than the latter. Commodus had been planning the gladiatorial games in his honour upon ascending the throne for the past five years. His one regret was that he hadn't written his ideas down and most he had now forgotten. Yes, he would definitely employ Titus as a chamberlain and secretary when he became Emperor.

There had been false dawns before but finally his father would meet his end. Commodus would allow him two coins for the ferryman, but the rest of the imperial treasury would be his. The wait would soon be over. But for Galen's miracle cures his father would have died years ago. Commodus inwardly cursed the priggish doctor, whilst conveniently forgetting that Galen had also saved his own life on more than one occasion.

Such was the Emperor's perilous state of health that the physician had warned Commodus, on his previous visit, that it might be his last opportunity to speak to his father. Aurelius had mustered his strength. He had first apologised again for not being as devoted a parent as he would have liked. Commodus had heard such words before though. When his father wasn't looking he had yawned.

Aurelius had then attempted to give his son one last lecture. He had quoted Epictetus, Augustus and, more so anyone else, himself: "Take care not to be too Caesarified and drowned in the purple... The first chapter of your life has been dedicated to pleasure. This next chapter that you are about to embark upon needs to be dedicated to duty, my son."

Commodus had nodded his head and looked dutiful – whilst vowing to himself that the next chapter of his life would be dedicated to tasting even more pleasures, carnal and otherwise.

The Emperor had also asked his heir to fulfil his father's last wish: "Promise me you will annexe and occupy this land. Finish off this war, in order to secure the peace."

"I will try father. But I now have a duty to the state, which must supersede my wishes. Should I lose my life or health while on campaign, how will I best be serving the Empire then? Even a good man can but change the world for the better gradually. But a dead man can achieve nothing. In order to truly do my duty I must return to the capital."

Commodus enjoyed the spectacle of a gruesome battle, as he also enjoyed the bloody combat between two gladiators, but he would rather not routinely spend his days ankle-deep in mud, surrounded by grunting soldiers. He would not eat second-rate delicacies, nor expose himself unnecessarily to injury or contracting the plague.

*An Emperor should sit upon a gilded throne in the Eternal City, not perch upon a wooden stool in a dingy tent.*

Rome was calling Commodus back home, as surely as death was summoning his father.

"Leave us," the adolescent suddenly said to Sabine, callousness replacing the surface charm he had exhibited the evening before. His capriciousness was his most consistent characteristic, the woman considered. She submitted to his request, glad to be out of his company. It was often an act of will for the courtesan not to shudder in revulsion or fear when he touched her. There was something abhorrent, rather than just depraved, about the youth. Sabine climbed out of bed, put on her robe and retreated to the room next door to the bedchamber.

"Stay," Commodus then ordered, turning to Titus. He wanted to discuss business and political matters with his chamberlain – matters which were not meant for a woman's ears, be she a whore or an empress. "Anything to report?" Commodus asked, as soon as he heard the door close behind the woman.

Titus' features quickly tightened in seriousness, as if he were a soldier standing to attention. He was the Emperor's agent as well as lover – and he would do well to remember that fact. Commodus had struck him with a centurion's vine stick the previous week for not remembering his place correctly.

"Aside from the issues we discussed before dinner I have heard a rumour that Rufus Atticus disappeared in order to locate one Gaius Maximus. Your father is apparently keen to see him. Whether for personal or political reasons, it remains unclear at present. Have you ever encountered this Maximus before?"

"I thought he was dead. At the very least he should be considered a condemned man. He was a centurion, one of my father's favourites – he trusted and admired the soldier. But five years ago Maximus murdered Pollio Atticus. It is likely that he also killed a number of the influential senator's agents, out of revenge for the death of his Christian bride-to-be. She met her god sooner that she had expected. Maximus was labelled a fugitive but was soon after pronounced dead by Galen, after a body was found in a fire. If Maximus does return then he will be given a hero's welcome by the army. My father will pardon him too. Certain factions in the Senate, particularly those who seek to prolong the war, may try to recruit Maximus to their cause in order to win support throughout the rest of the army. This cannot be allowed to happen."

As a child Commodus had lionised the centurion too. Maximus was the hero of the Battle of Pannonia and the boy would avidly listen to his father's stories about the officer's exploits, fighting the northern tribes. But Commodus also remembered how the praetorian often looked at him in disapproval. The lowly soldier also once dared to call into question his conduct during a fencing bout. The Emperor's son considered himself descended from Hercules, whilst the soldier's bloodline could probably be traced back to a pig farmer and a drab. Commodus had neither forgiven nor forgotten the transgression.

*I will not pardon him, like my weak father… Treat him as an enemy. Am I being paranoid? No. Or yes – but paranoia is a virtue in an Emperor. Better to be safe than sorry. History is littered with the corpses of trusting people. History will also be littered with the corpse of Gaius Maximus…*

## 10.

One of the Emperor's agents had arranged for fresh horses at designated towns to speed up the journey. They were making good time, traveling across the continent to Sirmium.

When and where he could Maximus conditioned himself; slowly but surely his paunch flattened out and turned into muscle. He also looked to sharpen his reflexes and skills by fencing with Atticus and practising on the bow with Cassius Bursus.

After fencing practise one afternoon, whilst their horses were rested and fed, Maximus and Atticus caught their breath in a clearing by a stream. The air was crisp. Woodland surrounded them but the bare trees let in a watery light. The sound of the fast running stream at their feet hissed, or shushed, them.

"What will you do with your pardon? Return to Rome? Live near Claudia and Marius?" Atticus asked his friend.

"I'm not sure yet. Rome doesn't feel like home anymore." The capital held too many bad smells and bad memories.

"I've been granted a pardon too, of sorts. I asked Aurelius if I could be granted an honourable discharge. My new life, so to speak, will start as soon as he passes away. He tried to talk me out of it but my mind was made up. I have no desire to serve under Commodus. Cassius will also be leaving the army. Aurelius has granted us all handsome donatives by the way. I should have no problem attracting a future ex-wife," Atticus joked.

"Do you have anyone special in your life at the moment, whether in Rome or Sirmium?"

"Maybe. It is winter after all. I need someone to keep my bed warm. But what about you? Did you leave anyone behind?" A smile softened Atticus' features as he thought about the enigmatic woman he was seeing. He couldn't altogether work her out, unlike most women, which made him want to get to know her all the more. At first their relationship had been professional and based on a mutual sexual attraction. But now it meant something more to him.

*Does it mean something more to her as well? Or are we just playing games, with ourselves and each other?*

"There's been no one since Aurelia." Maximus' voice was as cold as the icy wind which blew through the skeletal trees. He again fingered the gold band upon his finger, as he looked off into the distance, or into the past.

Flakes of snow began to gently fall and twirl in the gelid air. There was both a harshness and beauty to the scene before them. Either the world was due to freeze and die – or be renewed.

"You haven't asked, but there's been no one since you in regards to Claudia."

Maximus thought again about his friend's sister, the mother of his child. Claudia was startlingly beautiful. A siren. The soldier, or spy, hadn't needed to pretend to like her all those years ago when seducing her. There had been plenty of men before him. *What do I say to her?* He had used her that night. The fact that she was trying to use him at the same time brought little consolation. *She must hate me.*

"I was in love once, I think," Atticus said wistfully, breaking the silence between them. It was his turn to stare off into the distance. "It was before I joined the army and met you. I was just a teenager. Her name was Sara. She was a Jewess... We'd meet in secret. She was worth getting up in the morning for... She never bored me. I even had faith in the gods back then, believing that they must exist. Because she existed."

Maximus nodded, thinking about Aurelia and his first wife Julia.

"What happened?"

"Our parents found out. My father forbade me from seeing her – and Sara's father prevented her from seeing me. Shortly afterwards her family moved away from the capital. I always suspected that my father had threated their family, or paid them off, in order to get them to leave Rome. The son of Pollio Atticus couldn't be allowed to marry a Jewess, after all. It must have been a love story I was involved in, because it was tragic. We still wrote to one another but life ended up getting in the way of love. Her letters lost their perfume. Happy ever afters are like these snowflakes. If you try and grab one it'll just melt in your hand."

"You should watch yourself. You're turning into a poet again," Maximus wryly said, in an attempt to lighten the mood.

"There's no fear of that. A poet's pay is worse than a soldier's. The critics can also inflict wounds that not even Galen has remedies for."

Their conversation was interrupted by the sound of bracken snapping beneath Quintus Perennis' boots as he approached.

"We're ready to head off again," the cavalry officer said. "We should reach Sirmium by this time tomorrow."

"That means we've only got a day to work our way through the remaining wine," Atticus remarked to his friend, raising his eyebrows suggestively.

"Some battles are worth fighting, even when the odds are against you," Maximus replied.

## 11.

*He's coming.*

The messenger had said that her brother – and Maximus – would reach Sirmium by the end of tomorrow. Claudia's heart quickened and she took a deep breath. She fixed her hair and straightened out her dress as if he were about to knock on her door within the hour. She had just put her son to bed. Claudia had thought it wise not to tell Marius that he would soon be seeing his father for the first time, for fear of Maximus somehow not turning up. The woman was no stranger to the unexpected, or to tragedy.

Claudia walked into the triclinium of the house that the Emperor had rented for her from Publius Aponius, a local merchant who spent his winters in Athens. The villa was homely as opposed to overtly opulent. She sat down on the sofa and clutched one of the cushions to her chest, desiring something to hold. The oil lamps illuminated the striking murals on the walls. One depicted Cleopatra encountering Caesar for the first time, dripping with gold and sensuality. The second painting she recognised as a scene from The Odyssey, when Odysseus reveals himself to Penelope. Claudia had been Cleopatra in the past. Her father had turned her into a spy and trophy at an early age. But she yearned to be Penelope. Faithful. Good.

Flecks of snow, akin to white ash, continued to fall outside. Marius had eagerly asked his mother if the snow would settle.

"I don't know," Claudia replied. The boy had more questions than she had answers for – and not just in relation to his father.

*There is so much I need to explain. To both of them. But not right away. Marius is too young – and he may not even want to speak to me. Does he still consider me an enemy of the state? Please don't let things be too awkward.*

She felt like praying. But instead memories eclipsed the will to pray.

Claudia thought again about those two nights, half a decade ago. The night they had made love and the following evening when he had betrayed her (and her him). And when he had murdered her father. That blissful night, when they had been together, had it all just been an act? Had she lied to herself, as well as him, when she told Maximus how she felt? When she had woken up next to him, the morning after, she had thought that it might be the first day of the rest of her life. But happy endings exist only in books or on stage, Claudia considered. But maybe she had found a portion of happiness. Marius made her happy, gave her purpose. Galen had warned her when pregnant that there was a risk to her own health, should she choose not to terminate her unborn child. "You may not survive the birth." But she was willing to sacrifice herself. "I want something good to come from my life," she had said determinedly.

Claudia tucked her legs beneath her and made a shopping list for her housemaid that she would give to her in the morning. Claudia would cook dinner for him. She remembered Maximus' favourite foods. The Emperor had provided a house for her and a number of staff, although Claudia declined some members of a retinue, including a cook and a tutor for her son. Claudia had taken charge of her son's education from the start. The so-called "best" tutors were often the strictest – and the cruellest. She preferred to adhere to the writings of Quintilian. *I disapprove of flogging. We must take care that the child, who is not yet old enough to love his studies, does not come to resent them. Studying should be filled with pleasures.*

There had been no one else since Maximus. Claudia had told her brother that she had not remarried because she already had a man in her life, Marius. But partly it was because she still had feelings for the centurion, even if he could never return them. *He had loved his wife, Julia. And then Aurelia… I was just the sister of his best friend. Or something more monstrous…* Claudia occasionally envisioned him returning to Rome or meeting him by accident (Rufus had long ago told his sister that his friend's death had been a ruse). Even if their night together had been founded on lies everything, everyone, seemed unreal compared to what she felt for Maximus. Men now just wanted her as a mistress rather than wife. She was the infamous daughter – and agent – of the treacherous Pollio Atticus. An enemy of the state. A piece of graffiti on the side of a tavern in the Subura described Claudia as "Ulysses in a frock", the name that Caligula had given to Livia, the scheming wife of Augustus.

As well as sparing Maximus five years ago Marcus Aurelius also resisted the calls to punish Claudia. He saw her as a victim, not an agent, of her power-hungry father. The Emperor had invited her to dinner shortly after Pollio Atticus had died and Maximus had disappeared."The difference between wisdom and intelligence is the difference between compassion and cynicism. There is nothing wrong with you mourning your father, Claudia, but his death may prove to be a turning point in your life. A moment when Androcles removes the thorn from the lion's paw... I know that you may not think you should have much faith in yourself at the moment, but I know that Rufus has faith in you. I do too... Waste no more time arguing about what a good woman should be. Be one."

*I've changed. Has he changed too? I just want him to see Marius.*

The snow continued to swirl about in the air, like petals in spring. On the one hand Claudia wanted the snow to settle, as her son would enjoy waking up to such a scene. But at the same time, if the snow settled, he might be delayed.

*But he's coming. What will happen when he gets here? I don't know.*

## 12.

*The following day.*

Via the power of the gods, or due to the Emperor's religious stubbornness, Marcus Aurelius willed himself to leave his bed. His two attendants had helped him rise – and they also propped him up as he shuffled across the room. The Emperor now leaned on the table and peered over a number of maps. Galen had tried to dissuade his patient from overexerting himself but the demi-god had his way. The doctor suspected that Aurelius didn't want to appear too weak in front of his leading commanders and officials. At least the Emperor had deferred to his doctor's wishes in wearing a fur cloak to keep him warm. Galen also insisted that the Emperor wear the garment as it disguised his emaciated figure. With a subtle nod of his head Galen had a slave move a couple of braziers closer to the Emperor.

The physician barely registered what his friend said, as he addressed his men. Anxiety lined Galen's features, like lines scored into one of the maps on the table, fearing that his patient might collapse at any moment. Galen noted the worry lines creep into Commodus' expression too, though his anxiety stemmed from the fear that his father may have been displaying signs of a recovery. The observant doctor also saw that Commodus had invited his favourite into his father's inner circle.

*If Commodus will be Caligula reborn, then this Titus may prove to be a new Sejanus. History seldom repeats itself in a good way.*

Galen sighed. He then turned his attention to the Emperor. Aurelius was mustering his bodily and vocal strength, speaking more forcefully now than he had done over the past two months.

"It's been confirmed through two separate pieces of intelligence. We know the location of Balomar. He is staying with one of his kinsfolk here, just behind enemy lines. Come the spring he will tour the territory to form another alliance of tribes against us. We must not allow him to do so," the Emperor exclaimed, pounding his fist on the table. He sighed (or wheezed) immediately afterwards, from exhaustion and from disappointment at displaying such frustration and anger.

"Balomar" was the one name which could test the equanimity of the devout stoic. The leader of the Marcomanni had been a thorn in the side of Rome for over a decade. He was behind the initial raids on the Empire, which had started the war with the northern tribes. Balomar was a clever – and brutal – commander; he had been the author of too many Roman deaths – soldiers and civilians alike. Balomar had also been the architect of numerous enemy alliances. The wars with the Iazyges, Quadi and Chatti – Balomar had blood on his hands in regards to all of them. Whether through threats or promises he was the only man who could unite the Germanic tribes against Rome.

*The bloodletting will only end once we let* his *blood.*

"Just give me the order, Caesar, and I will wipe him off the map," Helvius Pertinax remarked, glaring at the mark on the parchment where it was reported the barbarian was staying. Pertinax spoke from a loyalty towards his Emperor – and personal enmity towards the leader of the Marcomanni. Balomar had been responsible for the raid at which his nephew had been killed – eviscerated.

Whilst the other soldiers in the room sympathised with Pertinax's sentiments Commodus eyed the senior commander with suspicion. The son of a freedman, Pertinax had risen through the ranks (Commodus preferred officers to be high born). Pertinax was a popular and accomplished officer, to such an extent that Commodus needed to keep a close eye on him, or else certain factions in the capital could recruit him to their cause when his father finally died.

"If we send a large force then Balomar's spies will alert him to our presence and purpose. He will disappear again and we will have more chance of finding a satisfied Pict. He knows the terrain and he has too many allies in the region. No, less will prove more. We need to employ stealth, not might. The plan will be to just send a handful of men behind enemy lines with orders to assassinate Balomar by any means necessary. It may not be the most honourable death for a king but Balomar would slit all of your throats in the night in a blink of an eye should the tables be turned."

Heads around the table nodded in agreement. The Marcomanni had proved themselves to be as trustworthy as Carthaginians over the past ten years. They could sign a peace treaty with one hand whilst clasping a dagger behind their back with the other.

"Do you have anyone in mind for the mission, Caesar? Few in our ranks could be sure of recognising Balomar," Pertinax said, worrying that the wily Marcomanni chief might even employ a double to escape capture and death.

"I do indeed have someone in mind, Helvius," Aurelius replied, mustering his strength to raise an enigmatic smile. "An old friend."

## 13.

Claudia straightened her dress again and took a deep breath. She tucked her hair behind her ear and squeezed Marius' hand, from nervousness and out of affection. She had washed her son herself that morning. Marius had already been excited by the blanket of snow outside, but there had been wonder in the boy's eyes as she told him that his father was coming to see him that day. He asked a hundred questions, of which Claudia could only answer a dozen or so satisfactorily.

A freshly shaven Maximus came into the triclinium, accompanied by her brother and Martina, her young housemaid, who had greeted her guests at the door. Firstly Claudia was struck by how much Maximus had aged. She had always pictured him as his younger self, stuck in time, for so long. Still he possessed his strong jaw, and appeared tough. But Claudia had experienced the tenderness underneath too.

*Is he still the most honourable man I know?*

"Thank you, Martina. That will be all."

The maid bowed her head and scurried off towards the kitchen, turning her head to take in the handsome brother of her mistress one last time before disappearing.

Age has not withered her, Maximus thought. Her full length woollen dress could not disguise the lithe figure beneath. A pair of violet coloured silk slippers poked out below the hem of the garment. Claudia also wore a silver brooch, in the shape of a deer, which the Emperor had given her. Unlike before, when she had been a celebrated beauty and shaper of fashion in Rome, Claudia now wore little or no make-up. Maximus recalled a phrase from Ovid that Rufus had often parroted many years ago: *The best make-up remains unobtrusive.*

Both Claudia and Maximus stared at each other somewhat sheepishly. But their mutual awkwardness brought them together. The air was free from enmity. Maximus couldn't tell if his heart or head (from his hangover) was throbbing more. He half-smiled at the attractive woman from his past, the mother of his child. She smiled back, kindly – unaffectedly. Maximus had long forgiven her, to the point where he couldn't remember if he had ever had reason to condemn her. Her sins had belonged to her father.

And Claudia had long forgiven him. The centurion had been doing his duty – and had saved the city through his actions. Also, her father had been her jailor; Maximus had set her free. Claudia had rehearsed the scene of encountering Maximus again a thousand times before. But she couldn't now remember her lines.

A welcoming fire crackled in the hearth. Maximus' nostrils were filled with the smell of fresh bread and honey-glazed pork, roasting on a spit in the adjacent kitchen. His half-smile transformed itself into something more fulsome when he took in the child by Claudia's side, clutching her hand and skirt. He was sweet-faced and blue-eyed. Healthy and happy looking. Despite repeatedly planning what he intended to say to his son when seeing him for the first time Maximus was lost for words. Something swelled up in his chest. Pride. Happiness. Love. A combination of all three and more. Cicero needed to add another word to the Latin vocabulary to articulate how he felt. Tears moistened his once sorrowful eyes.

"Marius, this is your father, Gaius Maximus," Claudia said, fondly, as she let go of her son's hand. Tears moistened her eyes as well, for reasons that the woman would be at pains to wholly explain.

Maximus dropped to his knees. Partly he was overwhelmed and partly he wanted to come down to his son's level. Look him in the eye. The boy tentatively walked towards the stranger. Marius' unblinking expression and the tint of his hair reminded Maximus of his own father. The child glanced at his uncle, who smiled back at him for reassurance. Rufus nodded at his nephew, encouraging him to approach his father. Marius looked back at his mother and she too signalled to keep walking. The child scrunched his face up in slight confusion, endearingly and adorably. Claudia smiled – and commenced to laugh cum sob.

At first the nervous child slowed to a standstill – but then his sweet nature vanquished his shyness and Marius suddenly ran the final few steps and launched himself into the chest of his father. His tiny arms barely stretched across the soldier's broad chest but he grabbed Maximus' tunic and clung on. And Maximus wrapped his arms around the precious child in return, clinging on for dear life, as if he were embracing his future. Meaning. Hope. And partly Maximus thought of Lucius and imagined he was embracing his dead son, come to life.

"I should leave you all to catch up," Rufus remarked. "I need to catch up on some sleep." The centurion also thought about the woman whom he wanted to join him in bed. *I've missed her.*

"Are you sure you would not like to join us for lunch?" Claudia asked, thinking how it might be too premature to spend time with Maximus alone.

"I'm sure," Rufus replied, thinking how he wanted to skip straight to his dessert. "I'll call on you later. We still have to meet with the Emperor. He's expecting us. Duty calls."

## 14.

The snow gave way to sunshine.

Cheers stabbed skywards, along with spears, as Maximus entered the camp, accompanied by Atticus and Cassius Bursus. Word had spread throughout the legion faster than a pox that Maximus was returning. Legionaries who had served under him chanted his name and thumped their swords upon scutums to salute the centurion. Those who knew Maximus – or just knew of the legendary soldier – joined the throng around him. Jokes were traded, jugs of wine were shared.

"You look good, for a dead man," one veteran called out to Maximus, who had served with him in Egypt.

"We both know that the only thing that could ever kill me is your cooking," Maximus replied.

He was invited by half a dozen old comrades to join them around the campfire later for a drink and meal. But mainly a drink. The most frequent thing asked was whether the officer was coming back to lead them again.

"We'll see," Maximus replied, suggestively. His mind was closed to the idea of re-enlisting however. *No more*. He just didn't want to ruin the celebratory mood.

Titus was in the camp at the time and took in the scene and atmosphere. He knew that it was his job to report the news of the popular centurion's return to Commodus – and the army's reaction to it – but he feared he would put his master and lover in a foul and petulant mood if he did.

"Hail the conquering hero," Atticus remarked in sardonic good humour, not begrudging his friend his moment in the sun.

"Wouldn't you hail him too? He has, after all, conquered death," Maximus replied, winking, grinning and clinking cups with the centurion.

The air was soon clogged up with snow again, however, and Maximus' jubilant mood turned into mournfulness, as he turned his attention to visiting his ailing Emperor.

*

Sawdust was strewn across the floor to soak up the snow that visitors brought in with them. Braziers glowed and hummed. Maximus stood before the Emperor, who again was propped up in a seated position in his bed. As grey and white as a statue. For a moment or two Aurelius stared vacantly, listlessly, into the opposite corner of the room to where Maximus was. Oblivious to the soldier – and the world. Such was the stillness and pallor of the Emperor's expression that Maximus briefly considered that Aurelius was already wearing his death mask. Maximus also noticed the numerous empty phials of theriac scattered across the bedside table. His brow creased in worry at seeing his friend so frail, so diminished. During his time in Briton the praetorian had always pictured his commander at his best.

*Age has withered him... But it withers us all.*

"Thank you for coming Maximus," the Emperor said kindly, his expression softening into fondness and a smile as he turned to take in his old friend. "Britain's loss is our gain. What are your thoughts on the island and its people? I've heard conflicting reports."

"If Rome is concerned with bread and circuses, Britain concerns itself with beer and cockfights."

"Everywhere is different and everywhere is the same," the philosopher proclaimed, although he decided that that particular phrase would not be included in his book of meditations. "Please Maximus, come closer. Step into the light. My eyesight is growing as weak as my voice. Have you been able to see Marius yet?"

It was not just the oil lamps hanging overhead which caused Maximus' face to light up, as he beamed and thought of his son. After Rufus had departed Maximus had spent the afternoon with Marius. He had asked the boy about his studies and his home back in Campania. Then they had gone outside into the garden and Maximus had taught his son how to make and throw a snowball. "You should twist and use your whole body, it's like throwing a javelin." Marius had cheered and laughed with delight when he got one throw right and the missile soared over the garden wall. On subsequent throws he had imagined himself throwing a javelin and felling Rome's enemies. He wanted to be a soldier, like his father. Maximus had explained that he was now back, from a special mission that the Emperor had sent him on. He would explain more when Marius was old enough to understand. In the meantime he intended to live near his son and catch up on the time he had missed with him.

"Yes. He is a fine boy and in good health."

"And how is Claudia?"

"She is well."

Maximus refrained from giving voice to his thoughts about how well she looked. He had continually stolen glances at her across the table as they had eaten their lunch. He had forgotten just how beautiful she was. Maximus was taken aback too by how accomplished a cook she had become. Regardless of his heart, she captured the soldier's stomach. After the child's exhausting afternoon and a filling lunch Martina had taken Marius upstairs and the boy had quickly fallen asleep. Once alone Maximus and Claudia had spoken to one another in earnest.

"He's a credit to you. He reads his letters better at five than I did at fifteen."

"He wants to be a soldier, like his father."

"I'd prefer him to be smart and kind, like his mother."

Claudia had blushed – adding to her radiant expression.

"He still needs his father," she had replied, resisting from voicing the thought that she needed – wanted – him too. "Can you stay?"

"Yes. Now I've found him, I'm not about to lose him. I've been dead long enough for one lifetime."

"He'll be happy to know that you're staying."

*I'm happy too.* "I'm sorry that I've been absent Claudia."

"You didn't know. I don't blame you. I should be the one apologising to you for what happened five years ago. For who I was. I need you to know though, that I didn't have any part in what happened to Aurelia."

"I know. I do not blame you. But let us not talk about what happened five years ago. Let's look to the future and the next five years. Although I cannot quite get over Rufus' change of heart. He was married, twice!"

"Perhaps he realised that he wasn't getting any younger. He no longer had the energy to jump out of the bed – and the window – when the husbands came home earlier than expected."

Maximus smiled to himself, recalling Claudia's joke. He also recalled her comments about how supportive the Emperor had been.

"I am grateful for you having provided for Marius and his mother in my absence. Rufus and Claudia told me what you have done for them."

"I publicly condemned you and pronounced you dead – I felt that it was the least I could do. I regret my decision in not pardoning you immediately, Maximus. In engineering your death however, I helped to spare your life I hope. I was caught between the Scylla and Charybdis of the army and various senators, loyal to Pollio Atticus. His allies are now weakened or dead, his influence non-existent."

After he spoke Aurelius winced in pain – and Maximus was reminded again of his imminent fate. The soldier had spoken to Galen, before meeting with the Emperor.

"He will be fortunate to see the summer. Or rather, given the bouts of torment he increasingly endures, he will be unfortunate to live till the summer," the physician had explained.

Maximus saw the Emperor's armour and weaponry on the wall opposite his bed. His attendant dutifully polished the set every day, full knowing that his master would never be able to wear it again.

"I am a dying man, Maximus. No matter how poor my eyesight gets, I see that. Even demi-gods cannot live forever. But to study human life over forty years is the same as to study it over ten thousand. Dying is but a sleep, to which one never wakes up. I do not fear death, but I do worry about what might happen in this life to my friends, Commodus and the Empire."

The aged Emperor took rasping breaths, from anxiety and exhaustion.

"Would you like something to ease the pain?" Maximus asked, tempted to call for Galen.

"Yes. Kill Balomar. It's the only way to end this prolonged war. He's the keystone. Take him out and the edifice of any opposition will fall. He's been behind every broken peace treaty. I also believe he has encouraged some tribes to sign alliances with us, only to have them break the treaty at an opportune moment. I have recently received reports of his whereabouts, not far into enemy territory. His aim is to form a grand alliance against us in the spring. I believe that you can succeed, Maximus, where successive armies have failed. You are one of the few men who can recognise him – and kill him."

Maximus pictured the barbarian leader, as he had seen him across the river at the Battle of Pannonia. Muscular. Square-faced and bald-headed. Gesticulating and bellowing orders. The enemy claimed that Rome was guilty of telling scare stories for propaganda reasons, but Maximus had witnessed the results of Balomar's barbarism first-hand. Captured legionaries were decapitated or tortured for his amusement. Women and children were burned alive, under his direct orders. Maximus had had to cut free some of the charred corpses from the stakes himself in one village. Balomar was not even averse to butchering his own people, should they show any signs of colluding with the enemy. The warlord had been responsible for the deaths of countless friends and comrades. He was in some way responsible for the death of Arrian, Aurelia's brother. Should he form his grand alliance then he would be responsible for thousands upon thousands of other people dying.

*But this is now somebody else's fight. I just want to see my son.*

"I came back to be a father, not a soldier."

Maximus pictured Claudia, as she asked him about his plans earlier. She would rather him remain a farmer than enlist again. It would not be fair on her or Marius if every time Maximus left the house they worried about him not returning.

"I've no intention of rejoining the army, Claudia. I've served my time, done my duty. I owe a duty to my son and you now. Besides, the cook at the camp doesn't have your recipe for honey-glazed pork."

Aurelius sympathised with Maximus' plight, but still implored him.

"I can but ask rather than order you to accept this mission. It's a dying man's last request. I will reward you handsomely. You and your family will be provided for, for the rest of your lives... But you must kill him. Cut the head off the snake. Cut out the cancer in our lives."

The Emperor's rheumy eyes fixed themselves upon Maximus' face – and soul. For once, the stoic had briefly bared his teeth and snarled. He noticed the old man clasp the sheets of his bed. He was clinging to life, perhaps solely to hear from Maximus that he would fulfil his mission, as death clung to him too from the other side. There was delirium as well as desperation in his demeanour. The wisest person Maximus had ever known was, for once, being governed as much by hatred as reason.

He recalled his first real encounter with his Emperor, mentor and friend. Neither of them had grey hair back then. Maximus was a young praetorian, serving as a guard at the imperial palace. He would often observe Aurelius out the corner of his eye, or strain to catch whatever he said. Aurelius would walk around the palace late at night, seemingly in a world of his own – wistful or amused by a private thought or joke. Or sad, for reasons that only he understood. Yet when he would speak to anyone, whether it be an official or to a lowly slave, he would treat the person as if they were the most important thing in the world to him at that moment. Maximus admired his judicial judgements. Aurelius was free from being corrupted by wealth, or the malign influence of powerful politicians calling in favours. "Let justice be done though the heavens fall."

Maximus was walking through the palace one evening, on his way home from his shift on sentry duty, when he saw the Emperor walking towards him along the marble-tiled, lamp-lit passage. Maximus stopped and stood to attention as the seemingly oblivious man strolled past him. Yet Aurelius was not four steps away from the praetorian when he stopped and turned towards the soldier.

"You are Gaius Maximus, are you not?"

"Yes, Caesar," he had replied, his rod-straight spine straightening up even more. Although Aurelius had worn a calm, equitable expression on his face the young soldier had still feared he may have done something wrong.

"I have heard good reports about you, Maximus. Of course, everyone has a divine spark within them but yours may burn brighter than most. I have noticed you, standing at the back at the occasional judicial hearing and philosophy lecture I give. Did I say anything mildly interesting or memorable? I must confess I often forget myself what I say or meditate upon. I suppose I should start writing things down. Indeed, I will commence to do so from this evening onwards," he had remarked, pleased by his new found resolution.

The praetorian's palms had sweated, his heart had raced and his mind had initially drawn a blank in attempting to remember something he had heard his Emperor say. But, whether borne from a divine spark or not, a light had shone out in the darkness and Maximus had remembered a line from a lecture Aurelius had recently given.

"Each hour decide firmly – like a Roman and a man – to do what is at hand."

The following day Maximus had plucked up the courage to ask his future wife, Julia, out to dinner.

\*

After visiting Aurelius and downing a few drinks around a campfire with some former comrades in arms Maximus rode back to Claudia's house. He saw his son again and tucked him in, telling him stories about his time spent with the Emperor over the years. After Marius fell asleep his father shed a quiet tear in private, as he remembered his other children, Lucius and Aemelia, who had been victims of the plague.

*Sunt lacrimae rerum.*

The sound of a distant shutter slamming against its frame could just about be heard over the howling wind as Maximus, Atticus and Claudia sat in the triclinium. Maximus waited until after dinner to tell them about his meeting with the Emperor and his decision.

"But why does it have to be you? The Emperor should know, more than anyone else, how much you have sacrificed in the name of doing your duty." Claudia wrung her hands as she spoke. Anger eclipsed her exasperation.

Maximus had tried to explain that he owed the Emperor for providing for Marius, for pardoning him and that their financial future would be secure if he took on the mission. In the end, however, Maximus told the truth, as to why he had acceded to the dying man's last request.

"Because he would do the same for me if our positions were reversed."

*I owe him a duty, as a son does to his father.*

Claudia pursed her lips, for fear of raising her voice even more and waking her son, and merely shook her head. She then stood up. First Maximus and Atticus heard the sound of rustling silk as the woman walked out of the room (her brother had noted how his sister had put on her best dress for the night, or rather for his friend). Then they heard the sound of a slammed door, as opposed to shutter.

"If I closed my eyes I might well have imagined myself back home, being married to my second wife," Atticus said, trying to ease any tension in the room. "As long as you make sure you come back alive Claudia will forgive you. When do we leave?"

"I'll be leaving the day after tomorrow, with Cassius. I need you to remain here, Rufus. If something happens to me then you'll still be around to take care of Claudia and Marius. Besides, you've got more chance of cutting Balomar down with an insult than you have with a bow. Unless your aim has improved dramatically over the past five years."

"Just make sure you assassinate the bastard rather than try to be an emissary. The last diplomat we sent to talk to the Marcomanni was skewered by a captured ballista."

"Balomar's already dead. He just doesn't know it yet," Maximus said, with a determined look in his eye. Consciously or unconsciously the soldier gripped his sword.

Atticus had witnessed that look in his friend's eye before – and believed him.

## 15.

Marcus Aurelius gazed on vacantly, glassy-eyed, for having taken Galen's ever more potent theriac. He was sat on a chair at the head of the table. Occasionally the eyes of the people in the room would flit towards the atrophied Emperor but most squarely looked forward and focused on the task at hand.

The two agents who had composed the intelligence reports, confirming Balomar's location, briefed Maximus and Cassius Bursus. They provided maps and other useful nuggets of information. One of the agents, Vibius Nepos, would accompany the soldiers most of the way, as he was heading in the same direction into enemy territory on a separate mission. Vibius had served as one of the Emperor's chief intelligence officers since the beginning of the war. Despite his naturally duplicitous occupation Maximus trusted his character and information. Vibius was a Roman aristocrat with a talent for playing the role of a German merchant or Greek diplomat. The spy was renowned for his ruthlessness and sartorial elegance. He had a narrow face with eyebrows that seemed perpetually arched, in a state of scepticism or accusation. A charming smile nestled itself within a neatly trimmed beard. Maximus also noted the large signet ring on his middle finger, which was rumoured to contain a poisoned needle.

"We will travel by horse up until this village, but then it'll be wiser to travel by foot and avoid the main roads. You both have a rudimentary knowledge of the local language I believe?" the agent asked the soldiers.

Cassius Bursus nodded. He knew how to order a meal, drink and whore. To learn anything else seemed superfluous in the eyes of the optio.

"I know enough to get us out of any trouble, I hope. Though it may be the case that I know enough to get us *into* trouble. But the plan will be to avoid any locals where possible. And if need be, this will do the talking," Maximus remarked, clasping the handle of his sword. He also made a mental note to have

Atticus teach him a few more phrases that might come in useful. His friend picked up languages as easily as he seemed to be able to pick up married women.

"I'm happy for you to kill as many locals as you see fit, just so long as it means you kill your principle target. We may not get another chance. *Carpe diem*. Balomar will be travelling with a personal bodyguard of around twenty men. But he will be away from the rest of his army – and those veterans with him will be rotated into three shifts. Once you do the deed then your best route back will be via these tracks and roads. I will arrange for men with horses to be posted here..."

Commodus leaned forward and paid close attention to the map and briefing as the agent discussed Maximus' route back to the camp.

After the briefing – Aurelius gave a slow nod of his head to communicate that he was content – Vibius instructed an attendant to tell the slaves to start bringing out food and to pour the wine.

Lunch was a veritable feast – a non-stop procession of moreish delicacies: large cubes of ham dipped in honey and poppy seeds; wild boar sausages seasoned with pepper; pickled snails; red mullet on a bed of cabbage, lettuce and radishes; spiced figs; local and imported cheeses; honey-glazed game pie with pine nuts. A few keen gourmets stood near to the door where the slaves entered with their large pewter plates of foodstuffs, in order not to miss out on anything (and to secure second helpings before the servers disappeared back into the kitchen). The Emperor had made a special effort. Atticus later grimly joked that "it was like the last meal, of a condemned man."

Beer, as well as wine, was served. Toasts were made to Nemesis (the goddess of vengeance) and Victoria (the goddess of victory) to speed Maximus and Cassius Bursus on their way.

"The gods go with you," Pertinax warmly exclaimed, raising his cup to the soldiers.

Maximus lifted his cup up in reply but thought how he would have preferred the less ethereal figure of Atticus to accompany him on the mission.

Shortly after Maximus exchanged a few private words with Pertinax he was approached by Commodus. The young man was wearing an ornate breastplate covered in gold leaf and decorated with various medals and honours (which had been bestowed rather than earned). Suffice to say the uniform had seen more polish than blood. His build was sinewy rather than athletic. Maximus recalled how Atticus had once said that Commodus often had a "lean and hungry look about him", quoting Julius Caesar's comment about Cassius Longinus. Maximus had never been fond of the Emperor's son – Commodus had regularly questioned the centurion about what it felt like to kill or man or torture a prisoner, but when Commodus visited the frontline it would often coincide with a Roman victory, and many in the army considered the child to be a talisman. Over the years Aurelius would give his son various titles, to compensate for the lack of affection and attention he gave him.

"I wish you every good fortune for your mission, Maximus. For we know how fickle a mistress fortune can be. A man can be a hero one day and a villain come the morning. Or even, in your case, a man can be dead one moment and alive the next. But I am preaching to the converted. You have experienced more triumph and tragedy than most," Commodus remarked, overly gesticulating with his hands as he spoke, his fingers tickling the air as if he were a bad actor. Maximus could smell the wine on his breath – and also perfume on his skin. "I fear that we will soon experience the tragedy of my father passing away. But my grief will be tempered slightly, and my father will feel better, knowing that you will serve me as you served him. You are re-joining the ranks of the army are you not?"

"I am afraid that I am just enlisting for this mission. I have no doubt that you will be able to find enough suitable men to serve your ends."

"You should never say never, Maximus. Who knows how fortune may smile on you when I become Emperor. I am but asking for your loyalty now. As Emperor, I may demand it – for the good of Rome, of course. Remember that I have the right to do anything to anybody, to quote Caligula," Commodus said. His smile turned into a self-satisfied sneer. A sense of mischief and malice gleamed in his eye. The problem was that Commodus couldn't differentiate between the two.

"You would do better to quote your father – and learn from his reign – than you would Caligula when you become Emperor," Maximus replied, wishing that the young man would heed his advice, but believing that his words would ultimately be in vain.

"I will be conscious of being my own man when I commence to rule – and absorb the lessons of all the Caesars who reigned before me. Your loyalty to my father is noted though. In some ways you were the son he never had. And I imagine that in some ways he was the father you never had. Does a part of you wish we could swap places, Maximus?"

"I am about to venture into enemy territory, nigh on alone, in order kill one of Rome's most formidable enemies. Most might call it a suicide mission. So, in answer to your question, I wouldn't mind swapping places with anyone right now."

\*

After lunch Maximus spent his time saying various farewells. In some instances comrades looked him in the eye and firmly shook his hand or hugged him as if it would be the last time that they would see the soldier. Maximus also called upon Galen, partly to hear his latest prognosis regarding the Emperor and partly to say goodbye. The physician was in the middle of preparing a poultice for an injured legionary but, once finished, he sat his old friend down and spoke to him in earnest. Age and fretfulness bedraggled his appearance but there was still a kernel of vigour and conviction in his aspect and voice.

"Should the choice be between fulfilling your duty and dying in the process, or failing in your mission but living to tell the tale, I want you to choose life, Maximus. You have a duty to yourself – and your family – over that of some noble idea you have in regards to the Empire. The Empire will still be the Empire whether Balomar's head is on a spike or sleeping on a pillow the following morning. You are in credit with Rome, you don't owe it anything. And make sure you bring Cassius Bursus back with you in one piece. He shouldn't fall in battle – but rather he should die from a pox in old age, as nature intended. You should return for Claudia as well as Marius," Galen expressed firmly, remembering what the woman had said to him shortly before Maximus was due to return: *He hurt me. But he's still the only one who can cure that hurt.*

As the crimson sun sunk into the horizon Maximus looked in on the Emperor, to say goodbye. Aurelius was in bed, sleeping. He seemed at peace and Maximus didn't want to wake him. He gazed at the old man in sorrow and fondness, as if he were already starting to mourn him. Perhaps sensing a presence in the room Aurelius woke and turned his head towards the door, but Maximus was already leaving and his lungs were not strong enough to call the soldier back.

Maximus had said his most important farewell that morning to his son, however. He had hugged Marius for what seemed like an age and there had been tears in his eyes. The boy had sensed that something was amiss and had asked again about where his father was going.

"I'm going on a mission – to buy you a pony," Maximus had replied. "I'll be back in a few days, don't worry."

Shortly afterwards, outside in the frost-tinged garden, Maximus had met with Claudia in private. The wind had blown her hair across her face but it disguised her tear-soaked cheeks. She had tightened the woollen cloak around her shoulders, but shivered also in fear. In fear of losing him – and of telling him and not telling him how she felt. The woman's manner had been as frosty as the morning air, however, as Maximus tried again to convince her of the virtue of his decision.

Claudia had refused to say goodbye to the too dutiful soldier, having experienced a presentiment that, should she do so, she would never see him again.

\*

That evening Maximus dined with Rufus Atticus, in a cottage close by to the camp which the centurion had rented. Maximus cast his eye around the place. The main room served as both a kitchen and dining area. An oil lamp above them squeaked, swaying from the breeze which whistled through the shutters. Shelves, bulging with books, lined the walls – interspersed with some freshly painted murals of Italian pastorals. A marble bust of Virgil (a gift from Atticus' latest lover) sat on the table, next to a bronze stylus. The officer had started to write again, inspired by something – or rather someone.

Atticus poured out two cups of wine and sat down opposite his friend.

"Aurelius gave me this vintage, on the condition that I should save it for a special occasion."

"Well it could well be our last drink together."

"I was rather thinking that it was special due to it being our retirement party," Atticus wryly said.

Maximus duly smiled and clinked his cup, thinking how he shouldn't get too drunk as he needed a clear head for his early start in the morning.

"I'll drink to that. Aurelius may well pass away before I return, Rufus. I need you to be ready to leave as soon as that happens. Claudia and Marius need to be ready as well. Commodus is not to be trusted. He may well view us as possible threats to his regime when he gains power. Or he may prove equally delusional and consider us allies – and we'll never be able to retire. I have no intention of being his friend or enemy. I owe Aurelius much, but I owe his son nothing."

"I've already placed most of our money with a trusted banker, if that's not a too oxymoronic title. I agree that we cannot entirely predict how Commodus will behave, so we need to be out of the reach of his sword arm, so to speak, when the time comes."

"I'll drink to that too," Maximus replied, holding his cup aloft again and thinking now that he didn't need *too* clear a head for the morning.

## 16.

The trio of Maximus, Cassius and Vibius Nepos had ridden hard for the first part of the day. A light shower in the morning had kept the ground soft but then the sun was on their back and the temperature rose to take the sting out of the chill wind.

Nepos was dressed as a merchant, but he had dressed the soldiers up to look like a couple of German hunters. They wore thick woollen tunics, which had been re-dyed and patched-up from different pieces of cloth to look authentic. They also wore woollen stockings and hooded brown cloaks which could double-up as blankets. The hoods would also cover their Roman faces and haircuts.

"Better to be warm and uncomfortable than cold and dead," Vibius said to Cassius when the optio complained about the coarse goat-hair undergarment he was given to wear.

As they neared enemy territory Vibius took them off the main roads. Although the journey would take longer he led them through a narrow woodland trail. The branches of tall oak trees criss-crossed above the riders. Cassius took point and scouted ahead while Maximus and the agent followed behind.

"So how good a shot is our optio?" Vibius asked, conscious that the success of the mission might ultimately rely on the archer's aim.

"He's the best I've ever seen. He'll be able to hit his target from fifty paces."

"It will need to be a kill shot, a head shot."

"I know. And Cassius will be able to hit his target from fifty paces. Or more."

The agent raised his thin eyebrows in scepticism.

"You may yet accomplish your mission – and live to tell the tale – Maximus," Vibius expressed, although not entirely convinced by his words. Balomar had slipped through the net many times before – and there were more outcomes related to failure than success.

"Even if we succeed, do you think that it will mean an end to the war?" Maximus asked.

"No. The war won't end but the act may prevent the war from getting worse. Balomar can be seen as a German Mirthridates. Not only is he an inspirational figure for those who wish to defy Rome but the Marcomanni chief also has the power to rally other tribes against us," Vibius posited, sending another small prayer up into the ether that Maximus would succeed in his mission and rid Rome of the thorn in its side. The agent was as keen to retire as the soldier – and spend the rest of his days with his young wife at his villa just outside of Massilia. Friends suggested that the aristocrat should live in the capital and go into politics but the agent had experienced enough back-stabbing and bribery to last him a lifetime.

"Do you really think that one man can make such a difference?"

"Aurelius thinks so, given how much he used to praise you for the difference you made at Pannonia and also for saving Rome from the machinations of Pollio Atticus. You have made a name for yourself Maximus. I've even heard you called the 'Sword of Empire'. But names can be targets – and swords double-edged. When Aurelius passes away Commodus may see you as someone he needs to court, or eliminate, given your popularity within the army," the agent remarked, his eyebrows raised in a warning to the soldier. He was worried by Commodus' imminent coronation, for himself, as well as others. Vibius envisioned being summoned to Rome in order to compose false intelligence reports and extract confessions from prospective opponents of the new Emperor. Those who possessed various properties which Commodus desired would, of course, be most at risk at being labelled a traitor.

Before Maximus had a chance to respond to the agent Cassius Bursus came back down the track, his brow wrinkled in concern and his hand clasping his bow.

*

Four seasoned warriors, armed with an array of weapons (short swords, hand axes and bows), were positioned at a crossroads on the trail. Two stood beside a well whilst the other two were starting a fire. Their four horses were loosely tethered to a post in the clearing. The Romans watched the barbarians through the dense woodland as they pulled out some ham, bread and a jug of wine.

"It appears they may be stopping for some time," Vibius said, shaking his head and pursing his lips. "We do not have the time to go around them. It's doubtful we'll be able to bluff our way past them either. If just one of those men escapes then he could alert the nearest village. And they'll hunt us down like a pack of hounds, as well as have word sent to Balomar about our presence."

"Is this your diplomatic way of saying make sure you kill them all?" Cassius Bursus asked, retrieving an arrow from his quiver as he did so.

Vibius nodded.

"How good are you with that knife?" Maximus asked, referring to the dagger hanging from the agent's belt.

"About as effective as you would be drafting a peace treaty, unfortunately. But I've had some experience knowing where to put the pointy end."

"Let's consider it two against four then, Cassius. They're still better odds than usual. We've also got surprise on our side."

Shortly afterwards Maximus and Vibius were walking towards the crossroads. Maximus swung a jug of wine back and forth and swayed a little, pretending to be drunk. Vibius too sparked a light in his eyes and smiled serenely, as if half intoxicated.

Most barbarians from the northern tribes looked the same to a Roman: long greasy hair and beard; dull or ferocious eyes; dressed in furs, leather and adorned with crudely crafted pieces of jewellery. The four men that Maximus and Vibius were about to address did little to challenge their prejudices.

The warriors harboured their own distrust and prejudices too when it came to strangers and they rose to the feet, their hands resting on their weapons, as the two travellers approached.

"Afternoon friends, would you care to share your fire and some food in exchange for some wine?" Vibius asked amiably in their native language, slurring his words slightly.

Maximus grinned and held aloft his jug of wine as the largest of the barbarians stepped towards him. The heavy-set German nodded at the strangers and licked his lips at the thought of more wine. Hands retreated from weapons.

There was a dull thud, and a slight clink, as Maximus whipped his arm around and struck the barbarian around the side of the head with the ceramic jug.

No sooner did Maximus hear the sound of his enemy slumping to the ground than an arrow whistled past his ear. The shaft struck the barbarian to the right of him. Cassius had targeted the man's upper chest, to kill him quickly and puncture his lung, silencing any scream.

The barbarian to Maximus' left was rooted to the spot, in either shock or fear. The Roman drew his short sword from beneath his cloak, as the German struggled to free his hand-axe from his belt. But just when Maximus believed it was going to be an easy kill the barbarian suddenly launched himself forward, butting his chest like a ram.

In the meantime the remaining German had reacted quickly. The young, agile warrior had chosen flight over fight. He turned and sped towards his horse. Just as Julius Caesar used to mount his horse by leaping onto it from the hind quarters so did the barbarian spring into position. He swiftly wheeled the black mare around, kicked his heels into its flanks and galloped down the muddy track towards the nearest village.

Maximus was knocked to the floor. Winded. His sword fell out of his hand and he was unable to reach it as the growling barbarian straddled his chest and pinned him down. A pungent smell of sweat and rancid cheese filled the Roman's nostrils. The barbarian's bearded face was contorted in rage.

Cassius Bursus let out a curse beneath his breath. Vibius stood between the archer and his target. He was also conscious of the fact that one of their the enemy had reached his horse.

The barbarian had now liberated his rust-spotted axe from his belt. The warrior clasped one hand around his opponent's throat, choking him, whilst his other was raised – about to deliver the killing blow.

Death would swallow another victim (one victim meant as much as the next). But perhaps death should be seen as more of a release – salvation rather than damnation.

The blade buried itself between two ribs, and slashed open his heart. Blood drenched his hand. The agent was as clinical as Galen in inserting his knife into the barbarian. Maximus gave Vibius a brief – but sincere – nod of thanks.

The rage was extinguished from the German's eyes immediately and Maximus pushed the odorous corpse off him.

The centurion didn't need to give the order. Cassius had already run out from the treeline and raced to set the fleeing horseman in his sights. Vibius bit his lip in anxiety, knowing that if the barbarian escaped the mission might be as well be over. With every moment that passed doubt took a chip out of the hope that the praetorian would be able to make the shot. The plan would have to be now to give chase and pray that their horses were up to the task.

The bow creaked under the strain and, for once, the archer's arm twitched slightly. Cassius gently breathed out however, and the arrow whished into the air. He had aimed upwards, in order for the shaft to arc back downwards into the target. He was unable to aim too high however, for fear of snagging one of the branches which hung over the track.

Hearts stopped and an expectant silence filled the air for a second or two whilst the arrow was in flight. But hearts then started up again, beating fast in triumph, as the missile stabbed itself into the horseman's back. The warrior arched his spine and then fell from his mount.

Vibius slit the throats of all the barbarians. Maximus noted how the urbane agent seemed to perform the duty with a sense of relish as well as ruthlessness. The mask slipped and the soldier took in the wild animal, or rather man, behind it. The spy's plan was to make things appear as if bandits had slaughtered the warriors. Vibius took what little valuables he found on the corpses. He also asked Cassius if he was carrying any dice with him.

"Yes, why?" the archer asked.

"There's a group of brigands who operate in the region – and after each raid they leave dice on one of the bodies, to mark their territory."

Vibius left the dice on one of the corpse's chests – a Dog throw, as opposed to a Venus throw, showing.

\*

The three men rode hard through the forest. By dusk they reached a fork in the trail, where Vibius would have to go his separate way. Maximus and Cassius would now have to travel through dense woodland to remain off the map, so the agent took all the horses with him. He would be able to play his part and blend in more easily, without being hampered by the soldiers.

"What's your mission?" the archer asked as they were parting, intrigued.

"There are some affairs – not just extra marital ones – that are best left secret. If I told you I could compromise both of us, should you be captured. I know from experience, people always talk. Especially when I ask the questions," the agent remarked, his mouth turned upwards in a smile, like a curved blade, as he remembered his last torture session.

"Well good fortune go with you," Cassius replied, thinking that he never wanted to get on the wrong side of the cold-blooded intelligence officer.

"Good luck to you too," Vibius said, thinking that, given the skill of the archer's aim, they had something even better to rely on than good fortune.

*They may yet complete their mission and live to tell the tale. But if I were a betting man…*

# 17.

Evening.

Lamps, braziers and candles were lit all around the bedchamber. Commodus' blond hair glowed in the light and he more than once admired himself in one of the full-length mirrors in the room.

*Give me excess.*

There were a couple of instances during the night when the wine-fuelled Commodus had believed that the figures in the murals decorating the walls were moving, swirling in a bacchanalian dance. Just after making love to Titus, however, his sense of revelry turned to paranoia. The figures were watching him, judging him. He blamed his headache on the painting rather than the wine. The classical figures, dressed in traditional Roman garb, represented propriety, virtue and his father. He was tempted to order his attendants to paint over all the faces, or just the eyes, in the morning. Or he would commission new pictures – of Dionysus, Hercules and Priapus.

*I have the right to do anything to anybody.*

Commodus and Titus lay on the bed, still a little breathless. Commodus wore a silk nightshirt dyed purple, inlaid with gold thread and studded with precious stones. He liked the feel of the material on his skin – and it amused him when the gems would scratch and cut his lovers as he writhed upon them. Titus was naked, marked with such scratches and cuts. Commodus had been rough with him earlier in other ways – but the would-be chamberlain did not dare complain.

Commodus had dismissed Sabine earlier in the evening. "I'm not in the mood for you tonight," the haughty adolescent explained, affecting a yawn. *She now bores me, like my wife does.* The courtesan had bowed her head and gone into the next room. She would return if called for, as Commodus had instructed her not to leave the house.

The Emperor-in-waiting blindly reached over to the bedside table, knocking a half-eaten plate of oysters onto the floor, and grasped a golden goblet of wine. Some of the ruby-red vintage ran down his chin as he gulped it down.

His eyelids were half-closed and he lazily dreamt of the gladiatorial games he would soon put on.

*I will mint new coins for the occasion, proclaiming a new golden age. Already I am called Germanicus and Augustus. But I will add to my titles, to add to my majesty: Pacifier of the Whole Earth, Invincible, the Roman Hercules... Lions will fight tigers, bears will fight drugged-up elephants. I'll order Galen to publicly dissect any exotic beasts afterwards, what's left of them. Blood will flow and cheers will rise up, alerting the gods to the earthly spectacle too. Dancing girls will fill up the arena between bouts... I will even fight myself – and break all records for a left-handed gladiator. I will fight as a dimacharerus – compelled to attack. And my enemies shall play the part of Hannibal, Spartacus and Catiline... People will remember the games. They will remember me. And love me...*

"Have you recruited the necessary men and briefed them, to deal with the great hero Maximus?"

"It's done, Caesar," Titus replied. Commodus nodded – in approval and because he liked it when people called him Caesar.

"My father will have some company when he meets the ferryman."

"Two dozen mercenaries will ride out and post themselves at the ambush point. If Maximus and the archer somehow complete their mission and make it back through enemy territory then Flavius Ducenius and his men will be waiting for them. Yet it may be the case that Balomar – and the enemy – will do our work for us."

"Indeed. But I must confess that I am slightly in favour of Maximus completing his mission and assassinating the barbarian king. I have no desire for Balomar to prove as irksome to me as he has been to my father. Have you instructed the men to make it look like bandits? Should there be an investigation, or should the bodies be recovered, Caesar must be above suspicion. But mercenaries are not the most loyal and trusted creatures. Word, or rumour, may get out one day. We may have to also deal with Atticus at some point," Commodus remarked, nodding to signify that Titus should rub oil onto his chest, stomach and elsewhere.

"And what of Claudia and his child? Sons have been known to avenge their fathers," Titus said, thinking that he would slit the throats of the family himself if asked, to prove his loyalty – and love.

"It's only natural my friend – and to be admired. Though I must confess should someone now usher my father from the stage I would feel a sense of gratitude rather than vengeance. But we should just sharpen our blades, rather than use them, in relation to Atticus and the woman and child at present. We need to turn our thoughts to Rome, rather than this barbaric backwater. The fourteenth labour of Hercules must be to strangle out any dissenting voices in the Senate. My father compromised with the brood of prattling women too much. He listened to too many voices – and the Empire has been overstretched and pulled in too many different directions. I will listen to just one voice when I wear the purple: my own. Let them hate me, so long as they fear me. Caesar must be Caesar."

*

Darkness was legion in the forest. The sound of wildlife occasionally murmured in the background. The chill wind whispered too between the trees, as if gossiping.

Vibius had provided the soldiers with extra blankets before departing – and both men slept near to the fire – but the cold winter night still bit into the bones of Maximus. Yet his thoughts, rather than the gelid air, kept him awake.

*You were fortunate today. The German was faster and stronger than you. Five years ago you would have seen his attack coming and avoided it… Instead of retiring yourself someone else may well retire you… No man has unlimited reservoirs of courage and good luck. There are only so many battles a soldier can fight – and live through. You can't beat the odds all the time… The main thing is that I have provided for them. It's the least, or best, you could have done. Rufus will keep an eye on them when I'm gone. Claudia has managed admirably so far in bringing up the boy. What can I add? How much love have you got left in your heart, after Julia and Aurelia?*

Maximus pulled his blankets around him even more, after tossing another couple of logs onto the fire. Tongues of flames darted out into the night with renewed vigour. He envied Cassius' ability to fall asleep at will. He envied the fact that the optio had nothing, and no one, to lose. But then Maximus recalled an encounter with Aurelius. The Emperor had asked Maximus to join him in the garden of the imperial palace. It had been night time, but a balmy summer's evening. He had just received his orders: he would be posted to Egypt. Maximus had been in two minds about whether to ask Julia to marry him. He loved her but was worried that he might make her a widow within a month.

"I fear death, Caesar. For both myself and for her," the young soldier had confessed, confiding in the man he had increasingly considered to be a friend and father-figure.

"It is not death that a man should fear, but he should fear never beginning to live," Aurelius had sagely replied, serenely taking in the divinity of the star-filled firmament.

The following day, Maximus had proposed.

## 18.

A blanket of mist still hung over the scene at midday, enshrouding the forest, large stone cottage and rippling stream. The atmosphere was damp and would soon be filled with rain. Similar to Maximus' own cottage, back in Britain, the secluded property had an outbuilding which served as a stable and a number of wooden pens which contained livestock. Maximus briefly thought of his own farm again and wondered if it would be part of his future, rather than just his past. Would Claudia like to live there? *We would be out of sight and out of mind in Britain, in regards to Commodus.*

Maximus soon shook such thoughts out of his head however and refocused on his mission. Along with Cassius he peered through the trees on the other side of the stream. Two burly, fur-clad barbarians sat outside the cottage and played knucklebones. *Sentries.* Maximus had yet to confirm Balomar's presence but he was confident that the chieftain was residing at the house.

"What are the chances of you making the shot should the bastard poke his head outside of the door?" the centurion asked his archer.

"I'm too far away, this side of the stream. The wind and rain look like they're going to get worse too. We may only get one shot – and I need to make sure I can make it count."

"Then we'll bide our time and wait for the right moment."

And so the two soldiers waited patiently. A shower came and went, dissipating the mist. Cassius occasionally gazed up at the serpentine plume of smoke emanating from the chimney, imagining a roaring fire and hot meal. To help kill time Maximus asked his friend about what he wanted to do, after leaving the army.

"So what's your happy ever after?"

"I wouldn't mind opening a tavern somewhere. I'd spend my days asleep and my nights in the arms of different serving girls. I'd fill the menu with my favourite foods and bar tax collectors and politicians. I'd rather have lepers, plague victims and even Christians frequent my establishment over those cretins. Of course you and the rest of my friends wouldn't be allowed to pay for any drinks," Cassius said, with a keen and impish gleam in his aspect.

"I think I'd prefer being a patron to an investor. Do you not picture yourself being married?"

"I thought that we were discussing my happy ever after?"

"You shouldn't let Atticus' experiences colour your thoughts too much. If you find someone who makes you laugh – or fulfils you in a way that a serving girl doesn't – then you might want to share your happy ever after with her. You should consider being a father too. Children are worth living for – and dying for," Maximus said. His expression softened in fondness, thinking of Claudia and Marius. He also thought of Julia, Lucius and Aemelia.

"It seems like you may have already found your happy ever after."

Before the centurion had a chance to reply he was disturbed by the noise of half a dozen warriors filing out of the cottage. The long-haired, swarthy looking Germans carried spears, bows and jugs of wine. It was a hunting party – hunting both for sport and for an evening meal of wood pigeon or wild boar.

Maximus recognised the large, bejewelled gold torc which hung around the man's neck. The Marcomanni king had obtained the unique piece of jewellery through defeating a Dacian tribal chief in a duel. The distinctive, bald-headed figure standing on the other side of the stream was indeed the same man Maximus had seen all those years ago, standing on the other side of the Danube at the Battle of Pannonia. The warrior king had aged but his features seemed no less stern and brutal. Deep-set, cold, calculating eyes looked out beneath a pronounced, bony brow. A cavalry sword, with a silver pommel, hung from his leather trousers. The sword had once belonged to a captured Roman officer. Balomar had used the weapon to skin the man alive. Under the banner of a religious rite the chief had then cooked the heart of his enemy – and consumed it. The Marcomanni king had been the author behind too many Roman deaths. It was now time to erase his name from the land of the living.

"It's him," Maximus said to Cassius. The usually stoical soldier's face was twisted in a sneer of contempt. *He's already dead. He just doesn't know it yet.*

The two men playing knucklebones were ordered to remain at the cottage. Maximus spotted another five warriors – and a couple of women – still inside the house.

The six men – and their chief – walked over the narrow wooden bridge. They were now on Maximus' side of the stream. Some of the men joked and clapped each other on their backs, taking swigs from a jug of wine. One or two looked to attach their bowstrings, only succeeding on their second or third attempt.

"They're going hunting. It looks like they're half drunk, which will hopefully make our job half as easy. The plan is to kill them all. There won't then be anyone who can come back, sound the alarm and give pursuit. We may just yet get to live happily ever after."

*

The men were now deep into the sodden forest. Shards of sunlight cut through the canopy of trees, chequering the ground in patches of shade and light. The sweet smell of dew and pine laced the air. The ground was thick with ferns and shrubs, some waist high. The rain-soaked ground was also littered with weeds, mushrooms and spongy mosses.

The hunting party were about to split up, in order to cover more ground to locate their quarry. But the hunters were being hunted.

Maximus and Cassius had kept their distance. The carousing warriors had made enough noise – laughing, singing, shouting – to be able to be tracked by a blind man. The soldiers covered their faces and clothes in dirt to further camouflage themselves. Cassius' bow would be next to useless in the forest, so the centurion briefed the archer on taking their enemy out at close quarters.

"Come up behind the bastards, cover their mouths and hack through their throats as if you were starving and their neck were a joint of ham. Don't be put off by the blood that gushes out. Take it as a sign that you're doing your job properly. Just keep on cutting."

Cassius nodded in reply and drew his recently sharpened knife.

The hunting party split off into pairs, with Balomar making a threesome for one of the groups. They now concentrated more on their spears and bows than their jugs of wine. The laughing and ribald conversations ceased. The Marcomanni were now hunting in earnest. But so were the Romans.

Maximus decided to work his way left to right. There was now plenty of distance between the groups of barbarians, although they were still in yelling distance to each other. As it was most likely that the group of three would be able to sound the alarm to the others they would dispense with them last. By then there would be no one left to call out to.

Maximus and Cassius moved stealthily towards their targets. They kept low, beneath the eye-line of their enemy should they unexpectedly turn around. The focus of the warriors was to look ahead of them, but their ears were pricked for any sounds of birds or rustling through the undergrowth. Thankfully the soft ground suppressed the sound of their footsteps. Despite the cold air Cassius tasted sweat on his upper lip. He tried to control his breathing and move forward in unison with Maximus. They closed in and stood behind two trees. Their prospective victims were just a few steps away. The centurion communicated to the optio with a couple of simple hand signals that they should strike. The barbarians didn't even have time to turn around. Their eyes widened in shock and terror and they emitted muffled noises as hands covered their mouths. But then it was over. Blood splattered over the leaves of a fern and the bark of a tree. Blood warmed the numb hands of their attackers too. The bodies slumped to the ground, their faces already ashen.

Maximus and Cassius crouched down, silently nodded to each other and wiped the blades of their knives on the corpses.

*Two down. Five to go.*

The soldiers were soon stalking their next brace of barbarians. One of the Germans, Adalbern, walked with a limp, caused by an old war wound which ached even more in the winter chill and damp. Whereas his thick-bearded companion scanned for any movement ahead of him Adalbern often cast his eyes downwards, possessing a fear, irrational or not, of being gored by a charging wild boar. He attuned his hearing, far more than anyone else, to the sound of rustling leaves and bushes. As such he turned towards his attacker before Maximus had the opportunity to creep up behind him. Yet the centurion was still too quick for the barbarian. Adalbern's warning shout to his comrades got stuck in his throat, along with the praetorian's knife. At the same time Cassius came up behind his opponent, cutting through his beard and then skin. Blood, sinew and wiry hairs matted the optio's blade.

*Four down. Three to go.*

## 19.

Whilst the two warriors who accompanied Balomar were focused on the task of hunting – one stood poised with a spear whilst the other readied his bow – the Marcomanni chief turned his attention towards the quarry he had been stalking for the last decade: Rome. As much as Balomar had dreamed of Marcus Aurelius falling in battle, flesh dripping from his own axe, he was still content for old age and disease to kill off his enemy. Balomar permitted himself a smile, as he thought of Aurelius' successor.

*The whelp will want to run back to his whores and pampered life back in Rome. He will welcome the peace settlement that I will offer him – and he can even call it a victory if he likes. The cease-fire will allow us time to re-arm and recruit. The Quadi and Iazyges will also know that Commodus is no Caesar, or Aurelius. The philosopher learned quickly, as a general and diplomat. Before Pannonia he hadn't won a major engagement but afterwards he didn't lose one. But once I have united the Germanic tribes I will purge our lands of the Roman disease. Like Arminius at the Battle of Teutoburg Forest I will ambush and slaughter the enemy. I will force them back over the Danube – and the Rubicon. Should the gods be willing they'll drown in the Tiber too.*

*I will flay Rome's arrogant and decadent senators myself. They derisorily call the people parasites. But the politicians are the true parasites, feeding off the labour and taxes of the populace. When the time comes the slaves will turn on their masters. I will but light the touch paper... Any society where the men perfume and oil their hair – and where husbands own bigger wardrobes than their wives – deserves to be conquered... But should Commodus dare to carry out his father's wishes of extending the boundaries of the Empire then let him. Let them overstretch themselves, thin their ranks and extend their supply lines. Let them also reach the Carpathian Mountains and disturb the hornet's nest of the Goths. They will die a death of a thousand cuts… Once Aurelius' light is extinguished the Empire will decline and fall…*

The Marcomanni chief knew he would be willing to give his life for the cause, though, to date he had been more efficient at laying down the lives of others in the name of freedom and victory. Balomar was distracted from his thoughts, however, as a pair of startled wood pigeons darted out from the trees and he, along with his fellow hunters, tracked their flight. Balomar was further distracted from his thoughts by the sight of two men standing before him, carrying knives, purposed to attack.

For a moment time seemed to stand still – for the time it takes a man's breath to mist up and disappear in front of his face – as the combatants took in the scene and assessed whether to fight or flee. Eyes widened, then narrowed and glances were exchanged. Hearts stopped and then pulsated faster than ever.

The barbarian archer decided that he would fight. His bow, with an arrow already nocked upon it, creaked back. The shaft was lined up with Maximus' chest but just before the German could unleash his arrow the Roman launched his knife into his enemy's throat.

Witnessing his comrade fall the Marcomanni warrior, carry a hunting spear, decided that flight was preferable to fight. He turned and fled through the forest, abandoning his chieftain to his fate – with the intention of raising reinforcements back at the cottage. Cassius looked to Maximus, who signified for his optio to pursue the enemy.

*Five down. Two to go.*

They drew their swords. The afternoon sun fell from above, slashing the scene in light.

Balomar snorted and spat out a gob of phlegm. He sneered at his enemy to reveal two fang-like front teeth. He raised his cavalry sword, admiring its polished blade and highlighting its length, compared to his opponent's gladius.

"Do you know who I am?" the Marcomanni chief asked in Latin, rightly believing his attacker to be Roman. He surveyed Maximus, not recognising the ghost from his past. "You should be scared."

"I'm too excited about the prospect of killing you to have time to be scared," the centurion replied, taking in his opponent. Scars, like scratches, marked his bald head. Despite his age he was still in a state of good condition. *Don't underestimate his speed or strength. Let him underestimate you.* Despite a burgeoning beer belly Maximus suspected that there was plenty of muscle as well as flab beneath his furs. Maximus had heard rumours about the prowess and ferocity of his enemy. Balomar had, on more than one occasion, defeated rival tribal leaders in single combat. A merchant once told him that the accomplished warrior even kept body parts from his defeated opponents as trophies.

"Do you think you're the first Roman to try and put me down? I've chewed up and spat out more of your countrymen than your Subura has whores," the barbarian proclaimed, grinning at his own insult, hoping to goad his enemy into making a mistake. "I'm even tempted to take you alive, to have the pleasure of torturing you. I'll snap your toes off one by one and eat your comrade's heart in front of your face. I'll even stuff his balls down your throat. As a Roman you may even enjoy that."

"You certainly talk more than any woman in the Subura. But if you're playing for time, in hope that one of your men will come to your aid, you will be waiting quite a while. You're men are currently all rifling through their pockets, looking for coins to pay the ferryman."

The leer fell from the barbarian's face and he raised his weapon. Balomar stepped forward and swung his sword in one swift, fluid movement – taking the tip off a fern as he did so. Maximus just about blocked the attack in time – and those that followed – before taking a few steps back, out of the range of the long cavalry blade. The German's eyes were ablaze with hatred.

"Your time will soon be over. Rome's time will soon be over, too. We are now the master race."

Maximus continued to move backwards, as he formed a plan. It was unlikely that he would be able to get close to his opponent, given the chieftain' skill, experience and the superior length of his blade. The praetorian parried the next couple of attacks, but when Balomar swung his blade horizontally Maximus deftly moved out of the way of the blow, instead of blocking it.

The freshly sharpened blade lodged itself into the hardwood tree behind the centurion. The German's eyes were now ablaze with terror. Balomar looked to butt his opponent, in an attempt to buy time to retrieve his weapon, but Maximus saw the attack coming – and the result was that the Marcomanni king shoved his head downwards onto the point of the soldier's gladius. The blood-curdling scream emitted by the barbarian, as the blade sliced through the jelly of his eye into his brain, frightened the two spectating birds away.

"Master race, my arse."

*Six down.*

But was there still one more to go?

*

Wet leaves slapped against Cassius' body and face. His damp furs weighed him down, but still he raced as fast as he could, ducking below low branches and leaping over exposed tree roots, in an attempt to close in on his enemy. He carried his bow, having sheathed his knife, just in case a shot presented itself. The optio spared a brief thought for his centurion, hoping that he would best the Marcomanni king, but then he refocused. His lungs burned and he felt the blisters on his feet burst open. He would indeed leave the army with an honourable discharge once this mission was over. The only thing he wanted to chase from now on were barmaids. The foliage thickened and Cassius lost sight of the German's head bobbing up and down through the gaps in the trees. But he would soon be coming to a clearing – a make-shift campsite in the forest – where he hoped he could spy the German again. He could not let him return to the cottage and alert his comrades.

The barbarian jabbed his spear forward, slicing through the Roman's hip. He had concealed himself behind a tree, just before the clearing, waiting for his enemy to come past him. The soldier barely felt the initial sting of the wound but he soon realised its seriousness. Blood began to soak his goat hair undershirt. He felt woozy, weakened. His legs nearly gave way.

Both men panted, attempting to catch their breath, after their long sprint. The squat, pig-faced barbarian grinned at the would-be assassin, savouring the moment. He would have a trophy from the day's hunt after all. His countenance was slick with sweat and grime. A dog-tooth jutted out from his mouth. He spat out a curse in his native language.

Cassius moved backwards, gingerly. He was unable to run. A wounded animal. There would be no escape. He still wanted to put as much distance between himself and his opponent as he could, though. Where there's life there's hope. Cassius mustered what strength and concentration he had left and reached behind him to retrieve an arrow. The smile fell from the barbarian's face, his eyes widened in surprise and alarm, as he read the archer's intention. He thrust his spear forward and charged at his opponent, looking to skewer Cassius before he had the time to nock the arrow and pull the bowstring back. The optio ignored the sight of his enemy – and crimson spear tip – rushing towards him. He just had to get his arrow away – and firing his bow came as naturally as breathing to the archer. He did not panic. *The harder you practise, the luckier you get.*

The shaft sprang from his bow just in time and stuck into the barbarian's sternum. With what little energy he had left Cassius drew his knife and finished off the Marcomanni warrior by slitting his throat.

Cassius collapsed next to the corpse. Death was beckoning the soldier, too. Darkness closed in on him, as if he were wearing a cowl. The impish gleam in his eyes dimmed. His bloodless face began to shiver in the cold. The optio pictured his mother and father and thought how they would be proud of him. He had died in service to the Emperor. "It is sweet and honourable to die for one's country", his father had once told him, quoting Horace. Rufus would also send what gold he had accumulated back to his family, so they could live comfortably in their old age. Cassius, with the help of his centurion, had written a number of letters to his parents over the years, keeping them abreast of what was happening in his life. The soldier had consciously kept some things back however, not wishing them to worry too much about him. *I'll have time to tell them everything in the next life though.* Cassius also drowsily hoped that there would be taverns in the afterlife.

## 20.

"I deposited half the money with your agent this afternoon – and you will receive the remaining half on completion of your mission. We are paying you a premium to buy your silence, as well as purchase your services," Titus remarked to the mercenary, Flavius Ducenius. The two men, sat on their horses, were in a field a couple of miles north of the army camp. Ducenius' squadron of cavalry were encamped in a neighbouring field. Night was drawing in. Black and grey clouds marbled the sky.

"Don't worry, I've no intention of boasting about the fact that I've assassinated Gaius Maximus. Even my closest friends in the army might crucify me for such a crime," the mercenary replied. Ducenius was a former legionary who had served out his twenty-five years and – along with a number of other veterans in their mid-forties who had retired – was a soldier for hire. Ducenius was tall, formidable looking and dressed in a fine fur coat. His armour and weaponry were custom made. His line of work as a mercenary was dangerous, but profitable. He provisioned and paid his men well and in return they were proficient and loyal. Ducenius allowed them their fun – looting and taking women as spoils of war – but they always completed the job at hand first. None of them would hesitate if he gave the order to cut down the lauded centurion. His narrow, brooding, dark eyes took in everything but gave little away. "I met him once, years ago. He bought my men a round of drinks." *He's a good man.*

"With the money that we're paying you can buy your own vineyard when this is over. Don't let sentiment cloud your judgement when it comes to doing the deed." Titus viewed military personnel with a mixture of snobbery and fear. Yet he believed that people – soldiers and civilians alike – should start fearing him, given his closeness to the future Emperor.

Flavius Ducenius flashed a baleful look at the lackey, as he deemed Titus. He snorted and a globule of phlegm shot out of his nose and across the perfume-wearing agent, just missing him. The soldier had come across Titus' kind before, all too often. *Preening, conceited and cowardly.* Just because they spoke for important men, they believed they were equally as important as them. The decorated praetorian was worth a thousand of his ilk. But the fee that Titus' employer was paying was worth even more to the mercenary.

"Maximus may be a good man. But he's also a dead man."

\*

"You didn't think that I was going to pass on the promise of free drinks when you open up your tavern, did you?" Maximus said, as the optio opened his eyes.

The centurion had tracked Cassius' path through the forest and found him – wounded and unconscious. He quickly lit a fire to keep his patient warm. With supplies and knowledge gleaned from Galen over the years Maximus sutured and bandaged the cut.

Whilst Cassius remained unconscious Maximus concealed the bodies of the enemy, just in case their comrades came looking for them. They would now smell, rather than see, the corpses first if they sent out a search party, he fancied. Before hiding the body of Balomar, though, Maximus pulled off the gold torc from around his neck. At first he would show it to Aurelius, as a trophy and evidence of his death. But then he would sell the valuable piece of jewellery and use the money to buy Marius the pony he had promised him.

Cassius' right side was stiff and sore with pain, as if his hip were on fire, but the archer had endured worse over the years.

"Balomar?" Cassius said, asking after the fate of the Marcomanni king.

"Not even Galen could bring him back to life. But how are you feeling?" The centurion was fashioning a make-shift crutch for his friend as he spoke.

"I'll live. You should see the other guy though," Cassius replied, part smiling and part wincing in pain.

"I did. If we weren't about to retire I'd give you training on how to use a sword and spear though. Are you fit to walk?"

"Yes, just about, I think. Although it may be some time before I'll be ready to chase barmaids again."

"With the war wound you've just received – and the reward Aurelius will give us for killing an enemy of Rome – the barmaids will be chasing you from now on."

"Now there's a happy ever after I can definitely relate to."

## 21.

Sentiment wouldn't cloud his judgement, Flavius Ducenius thought to himself, recalling the lackey's comment, as he peered through the treeline, waiting for his target. Indeed the chief sentiment the mercenary was governed by was a love of money. Ducenius pictured Titus again, his haughty demeanour and hair slick with myrrh. Perhaps the young lackey would one day climb the greasy pole of politics and be able to make policy. Ducenius had every confidence in Titus' ability to give an incompetent order to advance when an army should withdraw, or vice-versa. Titus was also more than capable of offering or receiving a bribe too, to further his self-interest at the expense of soldiers' lives. *Politicians are politicians.* But hopefully Titus would make enemies during his career – and one day someone would come to the mercenary and pay him to assassinate the lackey. Ducenius considered that he may even offer a discount for his services, for once. The soldier gave little consideration, however, as to who wanted the centurion dead. Past experience told him that it could be a rival officer, a jealous husband, a scheming senator or a woman scorned. *Just so long as their money is good.*

Ducenius' men had made it to the ambush point mid-morning, having camped in the forest overnight. It was now late afternoon. The lackey had mentioned how the enemy might do the mercenary's job for him and kill Maximus (and the archer he was travelling with). If so then he would still retain half of the payment. The plan was to wait as long as three days for his target to appear. Ducenius divided his squadron into two watches, just in case the soldiers travelled down the road at night. And so half his force was back at the make-shift camp in the woods, nearby. They would be sleeping, drinking some watered-down wine around the campfire or sharpening their weapons.

Sleet filled the air. The chill bit hard into any piece of exposed skin. Unfortunately the squadron were fated to follow where war, rather than good weather, broke out. The track was narrow and isolated, perfect for an ambush. They kept watch in the shadows, inside the treeline. Occasionally, on rotation, men would retreat further into the forest to warm themselves by a campfire and down a cup of heated wine. During the afternoon a number of locals and merchants had used the road. A few carried provisions that might have helped to shorten the prospective long days ahead but, as Ducenius reminded his lieutenant, Otho, they were soldiers, not common thieves. Rome and the Marcomanni had made the lives of the local people miserable enough. The mercenary had no desire to add to their privation.

"What will you spend your share on?" the hulking, bushy-eyed lieutenant asked his commander. Otho planned to use his bounty to pay off his debts, caused by his love of gambling and investing in risky business ventures.

"After my wife and mistress spend their shares I might well be able to afford to buy a jar of the army's finest acetum," Ducenius drily replied.

"That's funny."

*I only wish I was joking.*

"Although I may now be able to purchase two jars of acetum," Ducenius said, his narrow eyes widening and gleaming like two silver coins as he spied Maximus and the archer slowly making their way towards them. The mercenary gave the order for his men to ready themselves and surround their targets, when he gave the word. They were not to engage Maximus and the optio though, until he said so. Ducenius also instructed one of his men to race back to camp and have the other watch come to him and bring all the horses. Their mission would soon be over and he wanted to ride back to Sirmium as soon as he could – and collect the second half of his fee.

Maximus quickly drew his gladius and his body became alert at seeing the first couple of figures appear from out of the forest. His shoulders slumped, however, when the number of men grew to over ten. Neither flight nor fight were realistic options.

Ducenius, his sword drawn, approached the centurion. He briefly took in the injured archer: his pale face and black eyes. Cassius grimaced in pain as he turned his body to take in Otho, who stood by the side of him with his spear raised. He was half-dead already, it seemed.

"I don't suppose that you're here to provide us with an escort back to the camp?" Maximus asked, as he surveyed the band of mercenaries who surrounded him. Some carried swords, some axes and some spears. They had the grizzled look of veterans about them. They would all know how to handle themselves. They had all killed before – more times than some of them had bathed.

"If I said yes, would you believe me? I want you to know that this isn't personal, Maximus. In fact, I would much prefer to kill the person who hired me, whoever that is, instead of a fellow soldier. But business is business. You won't be able to talk or fight your way out of this one. There appears to be little fight left in you anyway, by the looks of things."

"You might be unpleasantly surprised by how much fight there is still left in me," Maximus replied, sword in hand, mettle in his voice. Although it appeared that a strong gust of wind might blow Cassius over he still firmly held his knife as well as his crutch. The optio cursed the mercenaries under his breath – and equally cursed the unknown treacherous bastard who had ordered their executions.

Ducenius nodded at the centurion, in acknowledgement and respect. The mercenary had little doubt Maximus had the skill and nerve to go down fighting. It wouldn't be good for morale, or business, if he needlessly lost men.

"You have fought with honour throughout your life, Maximus. It is only fair that I offer you a good death. If you die like a Roman and submit, then I give my word that we will take your bodies back with us so your families will be able to observe proper funeral rites and grieve you. Should you wish to pass on any messages to loved ones I will see that they are anonymously, but safely, delivered."

Cassius thought of his parents. He didn't want them not knowing what had happened to him. He wanted them to be able to say goodbye. The soldier was also sufficiently superstitious enough to want to die with funeral rites, rather than die like a dog in a ditch.

Maximus thought of Claudia and Marius... The centurion had experienced a presentiment before setting off that it would be one mission too many. He knew his story wouldn't end back in Sirmium, Britain or Rome. Poets and philosophers may claim that life is a journey – but death is the destination. After Julia and Aurelia passed away Maximus frequently thought about killing himself, when the light didn't shine in the darkness. He bought a vial of poison, which he kept in a draw by his bed. There was nothing to live for. He also knew that death was the only way to find out whether there was a God and Heaven. And he could endure Hell if he knew that the people he loved were in Heaven. He had been either too brave, or too cowardly, to end things before. But he would now submit – as much as dying like a Roman meant fighting like one. Perhaps he was fated to meet the ferryman at the same time as Aurelius, seeing as their lives had been so intertwined. He would live on though, through Marius. The soldier wistfully recalled something Rufus had once said, quoting Cicero, and hoped that there was some grain of truth in it: "The life of the dead is placed in the memory of the living."

"This is one fight we can't win, sir. I would like my body to go back to my family, if that's alright with you?" Cassius dolefully remarked, as if already in a state of mourning himself. *Some battles are not worth fighting.*

"I understand. You can buy me that drink in the afterlife." The officer clasped a hand on his friend's shoulder and offered him a meaningful look that communicated more than anything words could say.

The sleet turned to snow, misting up the air. Plaintive birdsong warbled out from the whitening forest. Part of Maximus felt guilty, for being responsible for Cassius' death. Part of him was scared: he was about to die. Part of him felt angry: he wanted to kill the man in front of him. Yet the soldier was also slightly and strangely at peace. Finally it would all be over.

Ducenius smiled, but not too overtly, realising that the men would accept his offer. He would duly honour his promise and deliver their bodies – and any messages – to their families. He had given his word – and a deal was a deal.

"Happy ever afters only really exist in books anyway." The optio tried to muster a smile to accompany his comment, but couldn't.

"I'd ask you to grant me one last request as well," Maximus said to the mercenary. "I need you to get a message to the Emperor that Balomar is dead."

"I will do so," Ducenius promised, as he heard the sound of horses galloping towards him from behind. His men were keen to get back home too, he thought. *It's time to finish the job.*

"Any last words?" Ducenius asked. He planned to execute the centurion mercifully, efficiently, by stabbing him through the heart. Out of respect for the centurion's loved ones he didn't want to cut his throat or disfigure him. He would nod to Otho – and the lieutenant would similarly dispatch the optio.

*The hour of departure has arrived and we go our ways; I to die, and you to live. Which is better? Only God knows.* – Socrates.

"Yes," Maximus said, as a sphinx-like grin unexpectedly replaced the scowl on his face. "Here comes the cavalry."

The centurion recognised the distinctive polished helmet and red plume of Quintus Perennis through the wintry haze. His nostrils seemed to flare as widely as his large, sorrel charger's as the decurion rode at the head of his squadron. The mercenaries barely had a chance to recognise that the twenty strong horsemen were the enemy, as opposed to the comrades they were expecting. The battle could little be described as such; rather, it was a slaughter. Quintus cut down the first man he came to, slashing him across the chest (the gash ran from his right shoulder to his left hip). The next horseman, riding just behind Quintus, swung his sword low and sliced open a mercenary's stomach. His intestines spilled out onto the road as he fell to the ground. A high-pitched scream spewed into the air – to be closely followed by another, and another.

Maximus first attacked the axe-wielding enemy to the right of him. The pinched-faced mercenary at first squinted at the indistinct group of horsemen galloping towards him – but then his jaw dropped when the decurion finally came into focus. At that point the tip of Maximus' gladius whistled through the air and sliced through his chin, lips and cheek.

Given the shock he must have felt at the surprise attack Ducenius reacted quickly. He realised he still had a chance to kill the centurion, flee into the woods and collect his fee. He lunged forward at Maximus but the centurion managed to parry the blow, having just felled the axe-man. With his opponent over-extended and slightly off-balance Maximus counter-attacked. With a flick of his wrist the praetorian cut through the tendons of Ducenius' sword arm. His weapon fell to the ground and the mercenary let out a roar that must have shook the snow from the branches over his head. With his uninjured arm Ducenius looked to unsheathe his dagger, which hung from his belt. As he clasped the ivory handle, however, Maximus jabbed his sword point through the back of the mercenary's hand and into his abdomen. The centurion stood over the defeated Ducenius, gore dripping from his blade.

*It was nothing personal.*

Otho watched his comrades fall or flee, as they looked to escape the horsemen by disappearing into the safety of the forest. The pay was good, but not so good that it was worth sacrificing one's life for. It was every mercenary for himself. A sense of violence and vengeance welled in Otho's stomach, however. He would at least bloody his spear by skewering the wounded archer, who stood immobile in front of him. Cassius witnessed the intent in Otho's eyes. The only thing the optio seemed to have time to do was close his eyes and resign himself to his fate. Yet Cassius failed to feel the leaf-shaped blade of the mercenary's spear plunge into him. When he opened his eyes he saw one of Rufus Atticus' throwing knives protruding out of his enemy's shoulder. Before Cassius had time to then blink the flank of Atticus' horse slammed into the brawny mercenary – winding him and snapping his neck.

*

The enemy were slain or scattered to the four winds. Quintus Perennis still gave orders, however, to set up sentries and a defensive perimeter. Corpses littered the ground and ribbons of blood scarred the freshly settled snow. The cavalry officer dismounted and approached Maximus.

"It's now my honour to say I served with you, Quintus Perennis," the centurion said. "You have my deepest thanks. Perhaps you could fill me in."

"I think it's best if Atticus does so, sir, as I'm still in the dark as to some things."

## 22.

Evening.

A pair of owls, seemingly flirting, hooted to one another in the background. Tethered horses snorted, whinnied and swished their tails. A few of the cavalry remained awake and traded stories about the afternoon's skirmish. There had been a few injuries but thankfully they hadn't lost anyone during the fight.

Maximus and Atticus sat apart from the main part of the camp, around their own crackling fire, sharing a jug of wine. Maximus stared intently into the flames, perhaps wishing that the tongues of fire could speak and offer him counsel. And consolation. His body and soul ached as if he had been placed upon a wrack throughout the past few days – or decades. Atticus had just provided his friend with an explanation of events – and asked the question: "What do you want to do? Kill him?"

For once Commodus had had reason to be paranoid about the paintings on the wall staring at him, judging him. They had been. Or at least one had been, as Sabine had stood behind the mural and spied on the Emperor to be. The room in the house next to the large bedchamber which Sabine had retreated into was not, as Commodus thought, along the hall. But rather it was a secret passage running parallel to the wall of the bedroom. It was not uncommon for some husbands to install such chambers into their properties, in order to spy on their wives. Or, as Sabine knew all too well, some people just liked to watch.

The courtesan worked as an informant for Vibius Nepos, but she had recently reported to Atticus (who passed any relevant intelligence onto the spymaster, who was always conscious of thinking a few moves ahead in the game). The two agents became lovers – and then something more: friends. They shared a similar sense of humour and love of literature. Both parties harboured doubts – that somehow the other was just acting out a role (or that they were lying to themselves) – but both also nurtured a hope that what they had was real. When Sabine had heard Commodus and her brother discuss the fate of Maximus – and potentially Atticus – she knew she needed to pick a side and act. The following day the agent had located Atticus, although it took a frustratingly long time to do so, and Sabine had recounted what she had overheard the previous evening. Atticus in turn had tracked down Quintus Perennis...

Atticus' question to his friend, whether to murder Commodus or not, seemed to hang in the air like a coin toss. Maximus twisted the ring on his finger and thought of Aurelia. She was the reason why his soul ached so much. In her letters to him she had often quoted the Bible.

*Man is born to trouble, as the sparks fly upwards.*

The fire sent cinders spiralling into the night air.

*Is this the light shining in the darkness?*

"I feel like I've killed enough for one lifetime, Rufus. It's not that I consider that Commodus is any type of brother, but I do consider Aurelius to have been akin to a father to me... What was it you also recently said to me? It's preferable to have a bad Emperor than a worse civil war. The misery may well begin, rather than cease, at his murder. I've got enough blood on my hands. Like Cincinnatus, I should go back to being a farmer... It seems you have may have found someone worth spending your retirement with, too."

"That I have," Atticus replied, smiling. The expression upon his face, as he thought of Sabine, was one that his friend hadn't seen before. It mirrored that of when a younger Maximus had thought about his wife Julia, many years ago. "I'm using the logic of third time lucky and thinking of making her an honest woman – if that's not too oxymoronic a title."

The two soldiers continued to talk, laugh and finish off their jug of wine. They also finished off discussing their plans for leaving. They would ride hard for Sirmium at first light. Rufus would collect Claudia and Marius, whom he had moved into hiding the day before lest Commodus' enmity towards Maximus extended to his family. Rufus would also meet with

Sabine – and ask her to come with him. "If she says no then at least I can use my broken heart to start writing poetry again. But I need her to say yes. I love her," Atticus declared. It was only after saying the words that he realised how much he meant them. The plan would then be for them all to convene at the crossroads, west of the town. Before he could leave, however, Maximus would need to say goodbye to an old friend.

## Epilogue

Galen was under orders to admit no one, except the Emperor's attendant, Commodus and Maximus. Commodus had already left the camp before the centurion arrived.

Maximus entered the room. Lamps, candles and braziers lit the chamber yet there was an air of gloom which couldn't be totally expunged.

The Emperor lay in bed. His hair was brittle. Maximus remembered how Aurelius' once glossy curls, which had hung down over his forehead, had inspired a fashion in the capital for others to demand a similar haircut. Liver-spots covered his snow-white brow and the back of his claw-like hands. The light flickered in and out of his milky, rheumy eyes – like the oil lamp hanging over the door, which flickered on and off.

The Emperor had decided to starve himself, to end things. "I want to turn the last page. I'm no longer going to fight death. Indeed, that may be the best way to combat it."

Galen had still protested, arguing that his patient should still eat something. But the Emperor wryly replied, "I may soon be feasting on ambrosia with the gods. I wouldn't want to spoil my appetite by eating mere cereal and honey."

That morning Aurelius summoned his senior advisers and Commodus. The stoical Emperor asked them not to mourn too him too much and to do their best to advise and support his son.

"Here is my son, whom you brought up, who has just reached the age of adolescence and stands in need of guides through the storm of life. You must be many fathers to him, in place of just me alone..."

Both Commodus and the advisers had dutifully nodded their heads, but ultimately the Emperor's words would fall on deaf ears.

"It's done," Maximus declared, deciding that he would not divulge his mission in its entirety.

The Emperor raised a smile, pleased that his centurion had survived and that his enemy had, finally, been defeated. Aurelius briefly closed his eyes – in repose, pain, exhaustion or peace. "Thank you. And Cassius made it back too?" His voice was little more than a whisper, as weak as the rest of his body. The Roman moved closer to his all-too-mortal Emperor, to hear him better.

"He was wounded, but Galen says he will recover. The real pain will come from him not being able to exert himself in the tavern for some time."

Aurelius raised the corner of one side of his mouth, to offer up a smile. "Regardless of whether this conflict ends or not you must go back home, Gaius. Make a home, with your new family."

Maximus sat by his friend, clasped his hand and cried.

"I hope those are tears of happiness. For I'm going home. No one knows whether death, which people fear as being the greatest evil, may not be the greatest good," Aurelius said, quoting Plato, in an attempt to console his companion.

The centurion thought him the best of Emperors and the best of men. They spoke for a little while longer, as they reminisced and Aurelius asked Maximus about his son and his plans. Sensing the patient's fatigue, however, Maximus brought a close to their conversation. The praetorian's final duty was to ask his general about the watchword for the day.

He wistfully replied, "Go to the rising son. For I am already setting."

*

After leaving the Emperor Maximus encountered Galen in the adjacent room. Both men somehow knew they would never see each other again.

"You've proved to be the greatest physician of the age."

"Tell me something I don't know. My incompetent contemporaries have done their bit to grant me such a title, as much as I have earned it, however. But thank you… It is a curse and a blessing that I see most things through the prism of science and logic, Maximus. Like Aristotle, I'm compelled to classify. Yet it would be wrong of me to judge you as being just a former patient or colleague. I consider you a friend. You have also proved yourself to be the greatest soldier of the age, though I say this with the proviso that you must still retire. Find some peace."

Maximus at first clasped a hand on the old man's shoulder but then he embraced the haughty doctor. Galen, a stranger to displays of affection, screwed his face up a little and felt decidedly awkward. But he also found himself wrapping an arm around the soldier, to return his embrace. He couldn't bring himself to hug the soldier with both of his arms, though. *No, that would have been too much. Much too much.*

*

Commodus spent the afternoon planning his gladiatorial games and going through designs and fabrics for his coronation robes. His good mood was punctured, however, by the news that Maximus had survived. He petulantly ordered for all of his attendants, bar one, to leave his chamber. He screamed rather than bellowed. Titus stood before his master. He put on his best contrite expression, whilst cursing Ducenius and Maximus underneath his breath.

"I do not know how he escaped, Caesar."

"An adviser should come to me with answers, not mysteries. Now get out of my sight, while I decide your fate." *I'll spare his life. But I will not reward failure. The whore can find another patron... Yet I will still need a suitable chamberlain and lover when I return to the capital.*

The soon-to-be Emperor smiled lasciviously and licked his lips as he recalled a young Greek freedman he had encountered – Saoterus. *A very suitable candidate... I'll take him. I have the right to do anything to anybody... He will love me, as much as the people and history.*

*

Sunlight poked through the clouds. The snow had melted. Buds were beginning to flower on the trees. Colourful songbirds darted through the air in a courtship dance – or a game of kiss-chase.

Maximus stood at the crossroads, outside of Sirmium, with Atticus.

"She said yes, would you believe?" Atticus said, grinning like a teenager.

"I hope she makes an honest man out of you, if that's not too oxymoronic an idea," Maximus replied, pleased for his friend.

Whilst Marius showed his new pony off to Cassius in the background Claudia approached the two centurions.

"We should leave soon. Are you sure you're fine about coming to Britain? The weather's bad and the food's worse," Maximus remarked.

"I'm sure. I'll be able to endure the rain and the cuisine, just so long as we all remain together. Marius is looking forward to it as well. He's treating it as his first campaign with his father." Sunlight – and something else – radiated in the woman's eyes as she spoke. Claudia had wept in private, in relief and joy, on hearing of Maximus' return.

"Cassius will be joining us too. He says he has an itch to visit the island again. And if he can make money anywhere from opening a tavern, it'll be in Britain."

Claudia kissed her brother goodbye and wished him well, before returning to her son and offering him some riding tips.

"Don't wait too long before visiting. Among other things I need to thank your wife-to-be for saving my life."

"Don't worry, I'll visit soon enough. You may be interested in having me as a business partner by then – and also as a brother-in-law," Atticus said, with a suggestive gleam in his eye, as he noticed his friend gazing lovingly at his sister.

Maximus smiled, blushed and nodded. "Anything's possible."

## End Note

In some ways the sun set on the Roman Empire after the death of Marcus Aurelius. After the five "good" Emperors, as they are deemed, Commodus was a terrible leader and turned the clock back to the dark days of Tiberius and Caligula. Aurelius' greatest failing was choosing his son as his successor, one may argue. Others would argue that Commodus was, unfortunately, the only choice.

I have now written books on Caesar, Augustus and Aurelius. I hold the latter in the greatest esteem. It has been both a pleasure and a privilege to write about his life – and quote him.

As always thank you for your emails and letters. Please do get in touch if you have enjoyed reading the *Sword of Empire* books. I can be reached via @rforemanauthor and richardforemanauthor.com.

For those of you who enjoyed *Augustus: Son of Rome* you may be pleased to know that I have finally started working on the sequel, *Augustus: Son of Caesar*.

Richard Foreman.

Printed in Great Britain
by Amazon